HERGÉ

★

THE ADVENTURES OF

TINTIN

★

EXPLORERS ON THE MOON

EGMONT

The TINTIN books are published in the following languages:

Alsacien	CASTERMAN
Basque	ELKAR
Bengali	ANANDA
Bernese	EMMENTALER DRUCK
Breton	AN HERE
Catalan	CASTERMAN
Chinese	CASTERMAN/CHINA CHILDREN PUBLISHING
Corsican	CASTERMAN
Danish	CARLSEN
Dutch	CASTERMAN
English	EGMONT UK LTD/LITTLE, BROWN & CO.
Esperanto	ESPERANTIX/CASTERMAN
Finnish	OTAVA
French	CASTERMAN
Gallo	RUE DES SCRIBES
Gaumais	CASTERMAN
German	CARLSEN
Greek	CASTERMAN
Hebrew	MIZRAHI
Indonesian	INDIRA
Italian	CASTERMAN
Japanese	FUKUINKAN
Korean	CASTERMAN/SOL
Latin	ELI/CASTERMAN
Luxembourgeois	IMPRIMERIE SAINT-PAUL
Norwegian	EGMONT
Picard	CASTERMAN
Polish	CASTERMAN/MOTOPOL
Portuguese	CASTERMAN
Provençal	CASTERMAN
Romanche	LIGIA ROMONTSCHA
Russian	CASTERMAN
Serbo-Croatian	DECJE NOVINE
Spanish	CASTERMAN
Swedish	CARLSEN
Thai	CASTERMAN
Tibetan	CASTERMAN
Turkish	YAPI KREDI YAYINLARI

TRANSLATED BY
LESLIE LONSDALE-COOPER AND MICHAEL TURNER

EGMONT
We bring stories to life

First published in Great Britain in 1959 by Methuen Children's Books.
This edition published in 2011 by Egmont UK Limited,
239 Kensington High Street, London W8 6SA.

Library of Congress Catalogue Card Numbers Afor 17608 and R 122385

ISBN 978 1 4052 0628 0

Printed in China
13 15 17 19 20 18 16 14 12

EXPLORERS ON THE MOON

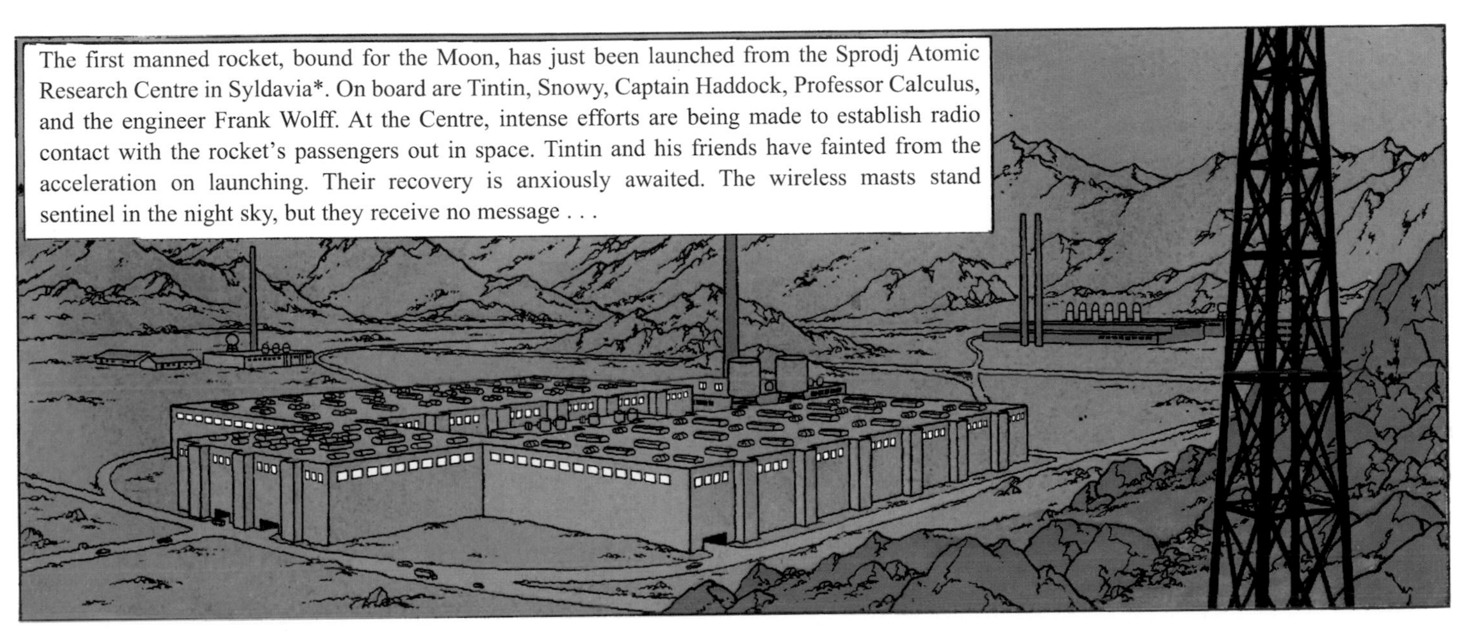

The first manned rocket, bound for the Moon, has just been launched from the Sprodj Atomic Research Centre in Syldavia*. On board are Tintin, Snowy, Captain Haddock, Professor Calculus, and the engineer Frank Wolff. At the Centre, intense efforts are being made to establish radio contact with the rocket's passengers out in space. Tintin and his friends have fainted from the acceleration on launching. Their recovery is anxiously awaited. The wireless masts stand sentinel in the night sky, but they receive no message . . .

This is Earth calling Moon-Rocket . . . Are you receiving me? . . . Earth calling Moon-Rocket . . .

Suppose we've made a mistake in our calculation! . . . That would be appalling!
Earth calling Moon-Rocket . . . Earth calling . . .

Meanwhile, unknown to the Centre, others far away are also listening in . . .
Earth calling Moon-Rocket . . .
By Lucifer, it's a bad blow for us if they're all dead!

* See Destination Moon

Earth calling Moon-Rocket . . . Are you receiving me? . . . Earth calling Moon-Rocket . . .
?

Moon-Rocket, are you receiving me?

WOOAH! WOOAH!
The dog! It's their dog answering!

Tintin! . . . Tintin! . . . Wake up!

Ah, he's heard me.

Snowy! . . . D'you want to . . . Why, what's happened to me? Oh yes . . . the launching, and that frightful crushing sensation . . . I was well and truly knocked out.

Earth calling Moon-Rocket . . . Are you receiving me?
Earth! It's Earth calling us!

Moon-Rocket calling Earth . . . This is Tintin here. I've just come round . . . I'll go and see how the others are.

I'm very well, thanks! But you aren't seriously trying to make me believe we're on the way to the Moon, are you?

Moon-Rocket to Earth . . . The Captain has just come round . . . Oh, and there's the Professor recovering . . .
. . . and Wolff too . . . So we're all safe and sound . . . What is our position please?

Earth to Moon-Rocket . . . You are now 2,500 miles from Earth. Your course is exactly as estimated.

Two thousand five hundred miles from Earth! Do you realise what an extraordinary adventure this is for us? . . . It's unbelievable! . . . It makes one's head spin!

Well, my head's not spinning, anyway! This whole thing is nothing but hocus-pocus and jiggery-pokery! You're just acting the . . . I mean . . . You're trying to pull my leg again!

So you doubt my word, eh? Well, you come up with me.

Golly! . . . Look over there!
!

Oh, so here you all are. . . . Whatever happened? . . . An earthquake?

Where in heaven's name have you sprung from?
From the hold. We decided to inspect the rocket before it goes. What's the time?

The time? . . . It's two o'clock in the morning!
Good . . . and the launching is set for 1.34? So we've plenty of time.

Plenty of time! . . . My poor friends, the rocket left the Earth half an hour ago. We are on our way to the Moon!

Ha! ha! ha! That's a good one! Always ready for a laugh, Professor!
To be precise: Ha! ha! ha!

Earth to Moon-Rocket . . . You are now 5,000 miles from the Earth. Your velocity is 6.9 miles per second.

This . . . this is a joke, isn't it? . . . You're just trying to frighten us? The launching really was fixed for 1.34?
1.34 a.m., yes! . . . Not 1.34 p.m.!

1.34 a.m.? . . . Not 1.34 p.m.? . . . Great Scotland Yard! We thought it was 1.34 in the afternoon!

Moon-Rocket to Earth. We have sensational news: the two Thompsons are on board. They decided to spend the night in the rocket, thinking the launching was at 1.34 in the afternoon.

But this creates a grave problem! We assessed our oxygen supplies for four people; now we have six on board, not counting Snowy. Will our oxygen last out?

You hear that, you brontosaurus? All this because at your age you don't know the difference between 1.34 a.m. and 1.34 p.m.!

Anyway, I must go up and take over the controls from the automatic pilot.

Blistering barnacles! When I think that I was forbidden to smoke one single little pipe, on the pretext of saving oxygen - the very same oxygen you two come here and gulp down! . . . And stop snivelling like that: you're making carbon dioxide! . . . Thundering typhoons, goodness knows why I don't chuck you overboard, without any more ado!

I say! Come and look! Come and look!
?
!

What is it?

Here! Come and look into this stroboscopic periscope: no human being has ever before seen this sight!

The Earth, our good old Earth, seen from over 6,000 miles!

If we have to die, it's worth it to have seen this!
Yes, I expect so . . . But personally, I'm in no hurry to die, if you don't mind!

It's a matter of opinion! . . . Now I'm going to take over control of the rocket.

Moon-Rocket to Earth . . . This is Professor Calculus . . . I have taken over control . . . All's well on board.

Blistering barnacles, that's enough moaning! . . . Now do me a favour and take yourselves off . . . I have important work to do!

Go on, hop it! . . . Get moving!

And you'd better not come down again till I call you! . . . See? . . .

And that's a fact! You need to be alone to study this sort of thing.
GUIDE TO ASTRONOMY

Now, let battle commence! To work! . . . To work! . . .

Earth to Moon-Rocket . . . You have just attained a velocity of over 8 miles per second. You are no longer subject to normal gravitational pull.

Now then, here we go! We'll tackle the first chapter.

Aaaaaaaaaaah! I've learnt something already!

Courage, Haddock! On to Chapter Two!

Sit down and watch. Look, there's the Moon in all her glory!

Is that really the Moon? That funny ball riddled with little holes?

It's amazing! Thompson, come and see this!

Mind out! Your stick's hooked up! For heaven's sake don't pull it! . . . Help!

At that moment, down below . . .
Here's to y-y-you, up th-th-there!

G-g-goodness g-g-gracious! . . . M-m-my whisky's r-r-rolled itself into a b-b-ball! . . . That's impossible! . . . Have I d-d-drunk too m-much already?

Too m-m-much or n-n-not . . . a decent whisky d-d-doesn't behave l-l-like this . . . C-c-come here at once!

W-w-whisky, stop f-f-fooling about! Get b-b-back in my glass this m-m-minute!
?

Blistering barnacles, what's the matter?

Something's happened: Snowy doesn't usually walk upside down like that.

Look what you've done, you idiot! You've stopped the nuclear motor. The constant acceleration of our rocket created a sort of artificial gravity here inside . . .

This allowed us to move about in the cabin as we do on the ground . . . When the motor stops, we no longer feel the effects of gravity . . . That's why we're floating like this.

Please, Professor, not a physics lecture now! . . . We must start the motor again!

Wait . . . I'll try to get to the controls . . .

If I touch you, Snowy, you're it!

Y-y-y-you see, my dear w-w-whisky! Y-y-y-you've t-turned yourself into a b-b-ball, but I'm a p-pretty little b-b-bird! Tweet-tweet! . . .
Tintin! Tintin! Where are you?

Watch out! . . . I'm going to restart the nuclear motor! . . . Hang on!

Carry on . . . We're holding tight!

L-l-look, Snowy! . . . I can even glide on my back! Th-th-this is f-fun!

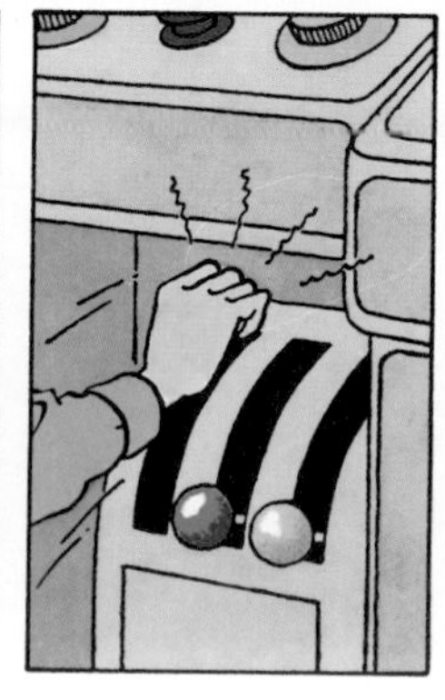

Earth to Moon-Rocket . . . What's going on? . . . Why have you stopped the nuclear motor?

Moon-Rocket to Earth . . . One of the two detectives accidentally closed the motor throttle . . . But we've just started her up again.

It's funny, we held on very tight!

Yes, but what to?

To be on the safe side I'm issuing everyone with magnetic-soled boots . . .

The Professor's right. If the nuclear motor stops again for any reason, these soles will hold us down to the cabin floor. Then we shan't float about like balloons.

Unless I'm dreaming, there's Adonis!
Who's Adonis? A friend of yours living near here?

The asteroid Adonis is a dwarf planet which orbits between Mars and Jupiter. It is a rock-like mass, about a mile in diameter . . . Take my place and watch, while I put on my boots . . . but for goodness sake don't touch anything!

There, that's that . . . But how do you account for one pair left over? . . . Has someone not put on his boots?
Crumbs, its the Captain . . . he stayed below . . . I'll take them down to him.

Hello, Snowy boy. Did you get very bumped about?
So there you are Tintin! . . . If only you knew what happened!

And the Captain? . . . Where's the Captain? . . . I . . . Hello, what's that piece of paper, there on the table?

Great snakes! It's fantastic! . . . He's gone out of his mind! . . . Quick, the Professor must see this . . .

Goodness! How lucky we put these boots on. The motor's stopped again . . . What's the matter this time?
RRRRING RRRRING
RRRRING
You see, Tintin? It's begun again!

Moon-Rocket to Earth . . . For some unknown reason the outer door has just opened. The nuclear motor stopped automatically. I'm going to see why . . .

Here's the answer! . . . Read this note I just found on the table, on the deck below . . .
?

"I'm fed up with your rotten rocket! I'm going home to Marlinspike." Signed: Haddock . . . Goodness gracious, then it was he who . . . Has he gone mad?

Mad? No, I think he's just soaked himself in whisky. In any case, we must look for him. If you agree, I'll put on my space-suit and go out myself . . .
Of course.

A few minutes later . . .
Moon-Rocket to Earth . . . The Captain has suddenly taken it into his head to jump out of the rocket . . . Tintin has gone out as well, to try and help him.
Ah, there he is.

Hello Captain! Hello! . . . Can you hear me?
Cuckoo, it's me!

Of course I c-c-can hear you . . . Can you hear m-m-me? . . . Tweet-tweet . . . Tweet-tweet . . . You see: I've turned into a little chaffinch . . .

Hello, Professor . . . Tintin calling. I can see the Captain. He's floating about ten yards from the rocket, going at the same speed as ourselves. I'll do all I possibly can to get him back on board . . .
All right.

Me b-b-back on b-b-board your beastly flying cigar? N-n-never in my life! I'm off h-h-home to Marlinspike!
But . . . Crumbs, it can't be true . . .

But it is! . . . He's getting further away from the rocket!

Poor Captain! . . . Now I see: he's being pulled into orbit by Adonis! . . . He's lost!

Hello Professor Calculus . . . Tintin calling . . . The Captain's getting further and further away . . . attracted by Adonis.

Getting further away? . . . That's only to be expected . . . He's become a satellite of Adonis!

This is terrible! . . . Surely there must be something we can do?
Of course . . . We must inform Earth at once, and tell them Adonis has a new satellite by the name of Haddock!

Not so fast! I have a plan: you raise the retractable ladder at once, so that I can anchor myself securely. Then, start up the motor: gently at first, but getting faster and faster . . .
But what are you hoping to do?

To get close enough to the Captain to throw him a line, and pull him aboard.
Pull me aboard? . . . Not on your life!

It's sheer madness! . . . But I admire you for wanting to try . . . I'll raise the retractable ladder as you said, and wait for your orders . . .

Tintin here . . . I'm securely anchored . . . You can start the motor . . .

All right . . . I . . . Tintin, it's terribly risky . . . But, good luck, anyway! Steady now: I'm starting the motor . . .

?

Tintin calling . . . I got a terrific jolt but I managed to hold on . . . You are right on course . . .

Yes, I can see the Captain . . . I'll close up to him. But for goodness' sake be quick. As soon as the motor stops Adonis will start dragging us into orbit.

I'll do my best . . . Steady now! Stand by to cut the motor!

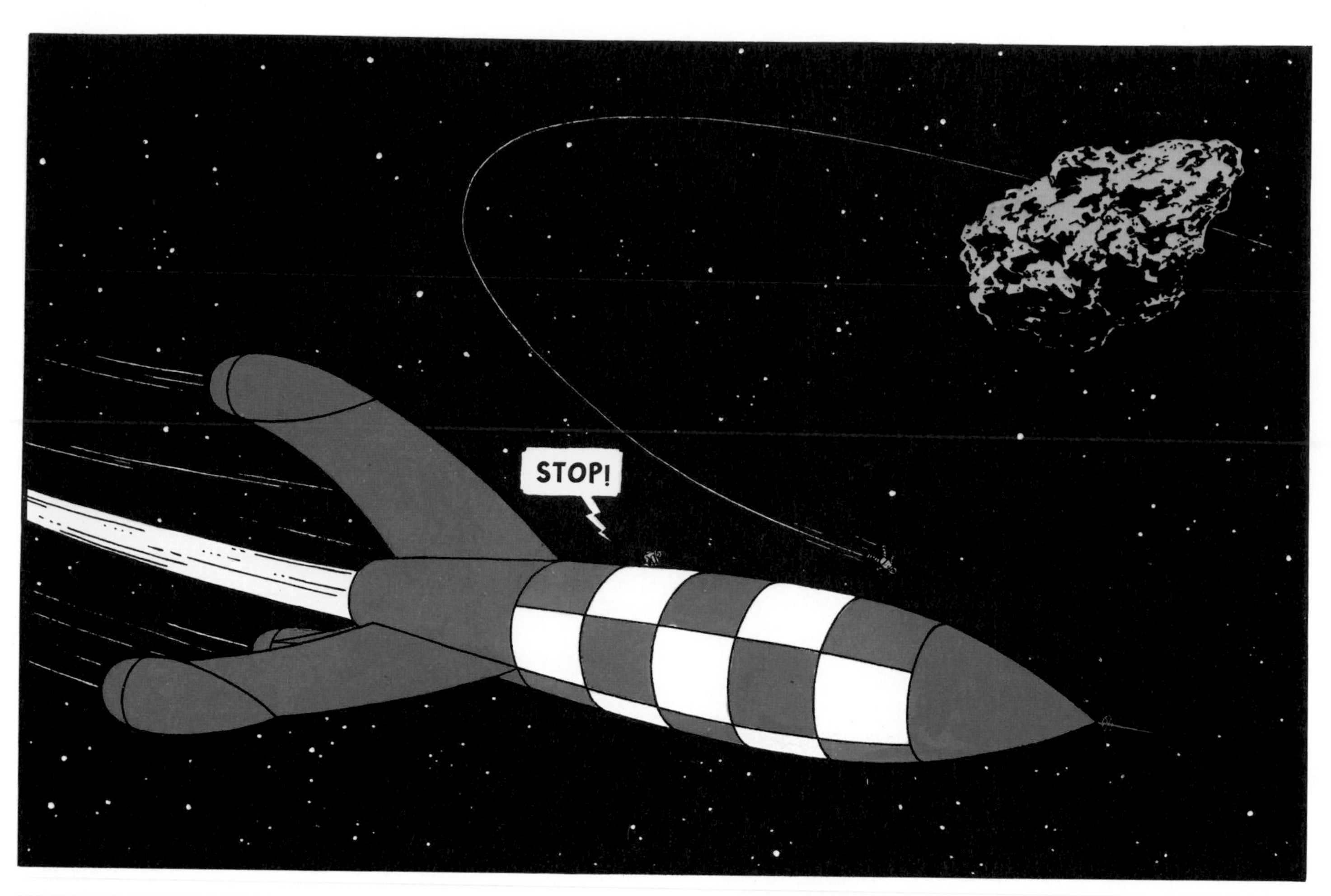
STOP!

A-roving, a-roving, ♩ ♩ since roving's ♪ been my r-u-i-n ♪
Let's hope I don't miss him!

Hooray! I've got him!
. . . I'll go no ♪ more a-r-o-o-ving ♩ ♩ ♪

Help! I've lost my own foothold! Lucky I'm anchored!

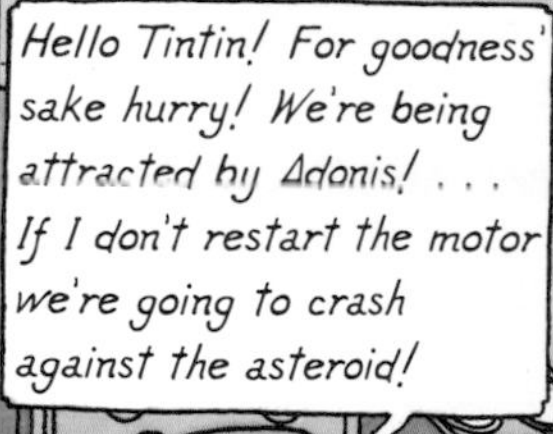
Hello Tintin! For goodness' sake hurry! We're being attracted by Adonis! . . . If I don't restart the motor we're going to crash against the asteroid!

Save yourself! . . . Save the rocket! . . . Start up the motor!
Blistering barnacles! What's all this rope doing?

?
Crumbs! What a jerk! . . . If only the rope doesn't break!

Hello, Tintin here . . . We're OK. The rope held!

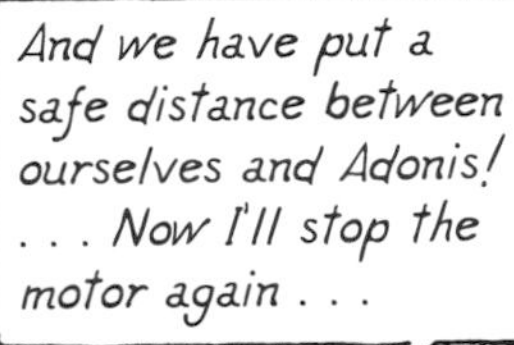
And we have put a safe distance between ourselves and Adonis! . . . Now I'll stop the motor again . . .

Saved! . . . We're just floating freely once more.

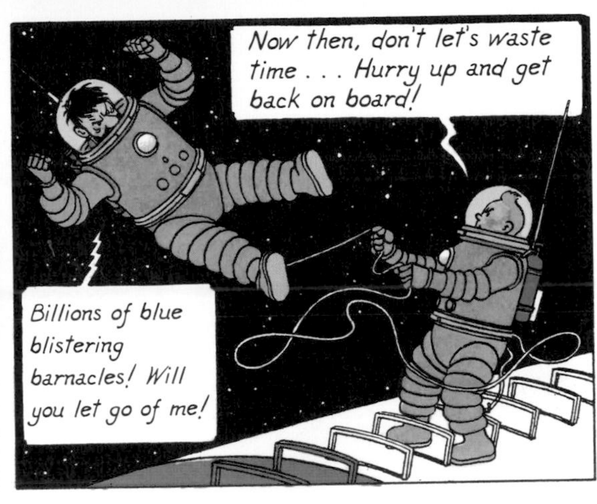
Now then, don't let's waste time . . . Hurry up and get back on board!
Billions of blue blistering barnacles! Will you let go of me!

W-w-w-what d'you think you're doing, eh? I'm quite old enough to d-d-do as I like! . . . I w-want to go home, so there! . . . I've had enough of this cake-walk, with whisky rolling up in a ball. We'll all end up smashed in little pieces!

Be quiet! Do you realise that all your tomfoolery has nearly cost us our lives? . . . Now we've had enough! . . . Get back inside at once! . . . And try to behave yourself properly! . . . D'you understand?

Now, come along! And if I catch you drinking again, I'll clap you in irons for the rest of the trip!

A few minutes later . . .
Moon-Rocket to Earth, Tintin and the Captain are safe and sound; they've just come back inside . . . We're restarting the motor . . .

I . . . I'm a miserable wretch . . . I had a drink . . . It's unpardonable . . . I'm terribly sorry.
That's all right . . . We'll forget it, but . . .

OH!
Well? What is it this time?

Tintin! . . . Tintin! . . . Come quickly! . . . It's huge yellow caterpillars!
?

There! . . . There! . . . Look!
!
GRR

But there's no doubt about it: this is hair!
It's hair?
?

Yes, hair! Great snakes! The detectives!
The detectives? What do you mean?

Oh dear, it's what I feared: another attack!

Yes, another attack . . . the trouble they developed after eating those strange pills in the Arabian desert . . . They've taken some medicine; we must wait till it works . . .
They always have to make themselves conspicuous, the jelly-fishes!

Yes poor fellows! . . . Are you in much pain?
Fortunately not: none at all.

OW! . . . YOW! . . . YEOW!
YOW! . . . OW! . . .

?
Oh, it's Snowy!

Snowy, let go! . . . No? . . . Then just you wait!

What are you going to do?
Fetch a pair of scissors!

There!

For the time being, until your medicine takes effect, I'll cut this shock of hair for you. But first let's go below; it will be easier down there . . .

Here, give me the scissors. I'll shear these merino lambs myself!
Oh? . . . As you please . . .

Earth to Moon-Rocket . . . Attention! . . . Attention! . . .

Earth to Moon-Rocket . . . Stand by . . . The turning operation will have to be made in twenty minutes' time.

Right . . . We're waiting for your instructions.

So now we're going to turn round . . . What's this latest acrobatic? Why not loop-the-loop, or do a roll, or go into a spin, thundering typhoons?! . . .
Wait, I'll explain to you . . .

BEEP . . . BEEP . . .

BEEP . . . BEEP . . . BEEP . . .
What in the world's that?
That? . . . It's a radar signal – a warning that a large meteorite is heading towards us.

BEEP . . . BEEP . . . BEEP . . .
Now we shall see whether or not the automatic system I installed works properly.
And how will you know if it works?

BEEP . . . BEEP . . . BEEP . . .
Oh, that's simple. The automatic system is controlled by the radar. If everything goes as I hope, then the equipment responds to the radar's direction signals, and prevents a collision with the meteorite. Otherwise . . .
Otherwise what?

BEEP . . . BEEP . . .
Otherwise, it's even simpler: we collide with the meteorite, and are completely pulverised!

BEEP . . . BEEP . . . BEEP . . .
But don't worry! We'll soon know!

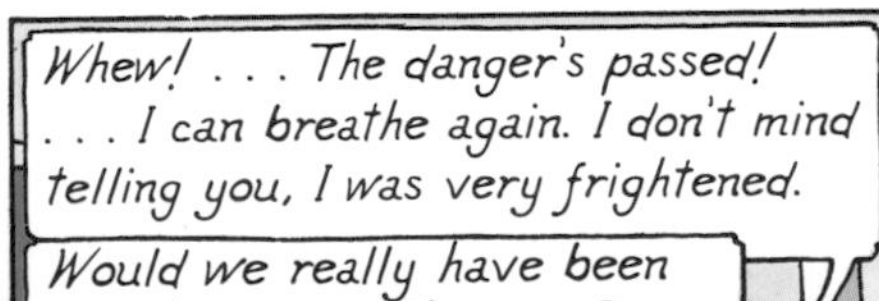

Whew! . . . The danger's passed! . . . I can breathe again. I don't mind telling you, I was very frightened.

Would we really have been smashed to smithereens?

Not only that! Far more serious! . . . I can tell you now: if my theories hadn't worked out, I'd have had to begin all my calculations over again.

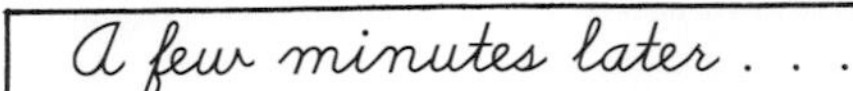

A few minutes later . . .

And when anyone asks me later on: "What was your job in the rocket?" I'll say, "Me? I was the hairdresser!"

A mop like this doesn't need a pair of scissors to cut it . . .

. . . it needs pruning-shears, ten thousand thundering typhoons, or a lawn-mower!

Whew! There's one cropped! Next gentleman, please! . . . What? . . . Is His Highness not satisfied?
Ha! ha! ha! ha! . . . My poor fellow! If you could see yourself!
?

Go on, laugh! Laugh! . . . If you imagine you look more dignified than your esteemed friend, you've got another thing coming!

And none of this would have happened, thundering typhoons, if you'd been able to tell the blistering difference between 1 p.m. and 1 a.m.!

There, that's finished! . . . Look at my hands now! . . . All covered in blisters!
?

Well, what is it? His lordship isn't pleased? . . . What more do you want? . . . A shampoo and set? . . . Or would you rather I put it in curlers?
OH!

Look! . . . There! . . .
?!
Ha! ha! ha! My poor fellow! If you could see yourself!

Professor! . . .
Professor!

Professor, we simply must do something for the Thompsons . . . Their hair grows as fast as I can cut it, and . . .
Ssh! . . . Earth's calling us.

Earth to Moon-Rocket . . . You have three minutes to go before the turning operation.
Right.

I didn't get a chance to tell you about this manoeuvre . . . What do you think will happen if we go on heading for the Moon, with our rocket pointing directly at it?
We shall end up by arriving, I suppose.

Of course, but like a missile. Travelling as we are, at such a terrific speed, we would crash on the Moon, and that would be the end of us all . . . Is that really what you want?
Me? . . .

Listen! . . . There's only one thing I want, blistering barnacles! To be able to breathe God's good air, instead of air out of a tin! . . . And to smoke my pipe! . . . That's all I want!

Good! Now, what do we do to prevent ourselves crashing on the Moon? . . . Quite simply, we turn our rocket completely round, nose to tail. To do this, first we cut out the main motor, and start up an engine giving directional thrust . . . Once the rocket has turned round, the exhaust from our nuclear motor will brake our descent. If all goes well, this will allow us to land quite gently on the Moon . . . You follow me? . . .
In fact, if I understand you correctly, it's the same procedure as for launching, but exactly the other way round.

Earth to Moon-Rocket . . . Stand by . . . Two minutes to go before stopping the main motor . . .

Get ready, everybody . . . And Captain, unless you want to start flapping about like a butterfly when the motor stops, hurry and put on your magnetic boots.

Oh Columbus! And my boots are down below! . . . Quick, I'll put them on . . .

One minute to go . . .

Thirty seconds to go . . .

Twenty seconds to go . . .

Ten seconds to go . . . Nine . . . eight . . . seven . . . six . . . five . . . four . . . three . . . two . . . one . . . ZERO.

I say, Captain! Did you have time to get your boots on?

Just . . . I've only got to do them up . . .
?

?
!

Earth to Moon-Rocket . . . Stand by to start up the directional thrust . . . Ten seconds to go . . . nine . . . eight . . . seven . . . six . . . five . . . four . . . three . . . two . . . one . . . ZERO.

Stand by to cut the directional thrust . . . Ten seconds to go . . . nine . . . eight . . . seven . . . six . . . five . . . four . . . three . . . two . . . one . . . ZERO.

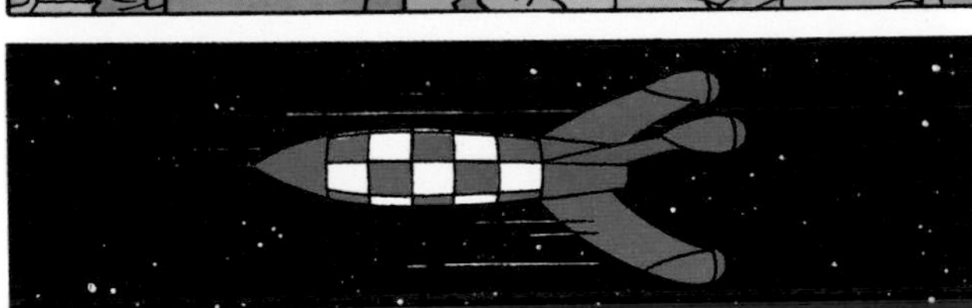

Stand by to start up the main motor . . . Ten seconds to go . . . nine . . . eight . . . seven . . . six . . . five . . . four . . . three . . . two . . . one . . . ZERO.

Moon-Rocket to Earth . . . The turning operation . . .

. . . was entirely successful!

. . . We are now in a position to reduce our speed gradually, and to land safely on the Moon . . .
Well, carry on, my friends! Happy Moon-landing! Ha! ha! ha!

I say, boss, do you really think they'll land on the Moon?
Ha! ha! I'm hoping so! . . . But whether they'll ever come back, that's another story!

I . . . er . . . don't understand . . . Why? . . . Is it . . . ?
Sh! Top secret! . . . You'll see later . . . Ah, there's their radio coming in again . . .
Earth calling . . .

Earth to Moon-Rocket . . . This is your present situation . . . You have another 88,000 miles to go . . . You are on the estimated course. You are gradually slowing down.

A little later . . .
Earth to Moon-Rocket . . . You have only 31,000 miles to go . . . In 40 minutes' time you should set the automatic pilot to land on the Moon at the selected place . . .

Moon-Rocket to Earth . . . Right! We're just going to have a meal now. Then we'll prepare for the Moon-landing.

Yes, my friends. If all goes well, in half an hour's time our rocket will come to rest on the Moon, on the spot I have chosen – almost beside the Sea of Nectar . . . Thank you, Tintin.

The seaside? . . . Why, that's wonderful. . . . It's ages since we went to the seaside, isn't it, Thompson?
It jolly well is! . . . But I didn't know there was a seaside resort on the Moon . . . Did you know that, Captain?

Of course! . . . Everybody knows! . . . I even heard that they need two Punch-and-Judy men on the pier. You'd fit the job perfectly.

"Lunar seas" was the ancient name for the dark patches astronomers saw on the Moon. We still use the names, like the Sea of Nectar and the Ocean of Storms. But you won't find a drop of water anywhere there.

The Moon is covered with high-walled depressions called craters. About 90,000 have been counted. Some are only a few hundred yards across. Others, like Bailly, measure 150 miles . . .
Gracious! Craters are hot places inside volcanoes. We'll have to take care that the rocket doesn't fall into one!

Don't worry; most lunar craters aren't live volcanoes. It's just the name given to them. As a matter of fact, we are going to land inside the crater Hipparchus, which is about 90 miles across . . .

No! no! a thousand times no! . . . I'm not letting that pass!
?

What on earth's the matter?
This . . . this man has insulted us, and we demand an apology!
Me? . . . I insulted you? . . . Me?

Yes, you sir! . . . Did you or did you not say that they need two Punch-and-Judy men on the pier, and we'd do perfectly for the job? . . . Isn't that insulting us?
Quite right! . . . This man has apologised to us, and we demand an insult!

No! You great oaf! You're back to front!
Oh? . . . You mean . . . we've insulted this man and we owe him an apology?

All right: I take back what I said. They don't need two Punch-and-Judy men on the pier: so you can't have the job . . . Does that satisfy you?
Yes, we're satisfied.
To be precise: we certainly are!

Yes, that's all right . . . quite all right. They don't need two Punch-and-Judy men, so . . .

So we can't have the job . . . It's simple, isn't it?

My friends! Calm down, please! Are the first men to land on the Moon going to begin by quarrelling?

Let us not forget that we are in mortal peril! We must keep our heads . . . Let us be friends . . . and restrain our tempers . . . Come gentlemen, make it up now . . . Then everyone must go to his bunk.

Everyone to his bunk? . . . But Professor, there are six of us, and only four bunks . . . Naturally I can give up mine to one of our friends here, but . . .
Certainly not!

Your place is at the radio: you must keep in touch with the Earth for as long as possible. I'll look after these two.

There are two spare mattresses: spread them out on the floor and lie down.
It's kind of you, but we aren't sleepy.

Sleepy or not, I say you're to lie down! That's an order, d'you hear? . . . An order!

It's time I went to help Wolff make final preparations for the Moon-landing.

Earth to Moon-Rocket . . . Stand by . . . Stand by . . . You are only 3,750 miles from the Moon . . .

Moon-Rocket to Earth . . . Right . . . We are making final preparations . . . The Professor is now setting the automatic pilot . . .

Another seven points East . . . No, that's too much . . . One point West, Wolff . . . There, that's it! The rocket is now heading right for the centre of the crater Hipparchus.

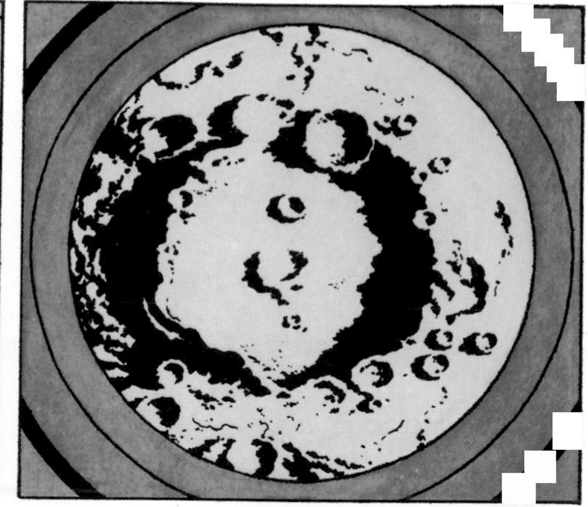

Here, Snowy!

You see, you'll feel much . . .

. . . better here while the rocket . . . I say! What do you think you're doing?

Us? . . . We're going to lie down like we've been told to! . . . But my colleague and I don't sleep in our clothes.

Blistering barnacles! You don't have to sleep, you prize purple jelly-fishes! You were told to lie down. That's all! So jump to it!

And get a move on, you dunder-headed Ethelreds! . . . If the Professor catches you still around, he'll probably maroon you on an empty planet . . . Look, here he comes now.

Ah, everybody lying down? That's good. You must come now, Wolff.

Moon-Rocket to Earth . . . All's well. We are ready. The automatic pilot is set towards the middle of the crater Hipparchus. We're all lying on our bunks, waiting.

Moon-Rocket to Earth . . . The nuclear motor has just stopped, and the auxiliary engine has taken over.

It's amazing! . . . It's tremendous! . . . It's incredible! Just think: in a few minutes' time, either we'll be walking on the Moon, or we'll all be dead. It's marvellous!

Moon-Rocket to Earth . . . Tintin calling . . . We are beginning to feel the effects of slackening speed . . .

The rocket is being shaken by slight vibrations . . . We are lying flat on our bunks . . . It's an effort to make the least movement . . .

Our ears are ringing . . . The vibrations are getting stronger and stronger . . . The crushing sensation is worse . . . It's getting difficult to breathe . . .

We're being crushed into our bunks . . . by an intolerable . . . weight . . . can't move now . . . The Professor . . . blacked out . . . I . . . think . . . I think . . .

. . . my head . . . will . . . burst! . . . My eyes . . . I . . . I'm sure . . . they'll pop . . . out of their . . . sockets . . . I . . . My heart . . . Oh, my heart . . .

Hello . . . The Cap . . . the Captain . . . blacked out too . . . Ooh, this is agony . . . The . . . the rocket . . . shaking . . . in every rivet . . . Let's hope . . . Let's hope . . . it won't . . . Oooh!

. . . . errr . . . .
. . . ftttt . . . .
. . . . crrr . . . . .

That's all . . . Nothing more! . . . Poor Tintin must have blacked out as well . . . Oh, this silence is unbearable!

WOOW OW OW OW!!

WOOW OW OW OW!!!

That was the dog howling for the dead! . . . Then he must have passed out too.

Earth to Moon-Rocket . . .
. . . Are you receiving me! . . .
Earth to Moon-Rocket . . .

Crrr . . . crrr . . . crrr . . .
Earth to Moon-Rocket . . . Are you receiving me? . . .

Earth to Moon-Rocket . . . Are you receiving me? . . .

Earth to Moon-Rocket . . . Are you receiving me? . . .
By Lucifer! Let's hope nothing has happened to them!

Earth to Moon-Rocket . . .
Earth to Moon-Rocket . . .
Are you receiving me? . . .

Something must be wrong . . . We've been calling them for more than half an hour, and still no answer . . . Try again . . .
Earth to Moon-Rocket . . . Are you receiving me?

Moon-Rocket to Earth . . . Moon-Rocket to Earth . . . Receiving you loud and clear . . .
They're alive! . . . They're alive! . . .
Hooray!

This is Cuthbert Calculus speaking to you from the Moon!! . . . Success! . . . Success!! . . . We're all safe and sound . . . We couldn't get through to you before; the radio was damaged. It must have been the vibrations that shook the rocket . . . Hello Earth . . . Did you get that?

Message received . . . But it sounds as if the vibrations haven't stopped yet: we can hear strange rumbling noises . . .

I . . . er . . . It's nothing: don't worry . . . You can hear . . . er . . . the two detectives snoring! . . . They haven't woken up yet.
ZZZZ . . .
ZZZZ . . .

Now we are going to disembark from the rocket . . . The honour has fallen to the youngest among us: we have chosen Tintin to be the first human being to set foot on the Moon . . . He's just gone down to put on his equipment. He'll give you a direct account of his first impressions, so I'll hand you over to him . . . That's all for now . . .

This is Tintin speaking. I've just put on my space-suit and am now standing in the air-lock. They're just going to reduce the pressure to a vacuum inside here. Captain Haddock is in charge. I'm waiting for his final instructions.

Captain Haddock speaking . . Pressure zero . . . Retractable ladder in position . . . Are you ready? Stand by! . . . I'm opening the door!
It's a solemn moment . . . The outside door is swinging slowly on its hinges and . . .

OOOOOOH! . . .
?
?

Oooh! What a fantastic sight!

It's . . . How can I describe it? . . . It's a nightmare land, a place of death, horrifying in its desolation . . . Not a tree, not a flower, not a blade of grass. . . . Not a bird, not a sound, not a cloud. In the inky black sky there are thousands of stars . . .

. . . but they are motionless, frozen; they don't twinkle in the way that makes them look so alive to us on Earth.

Now I'm descending the ladder which runs down the side of the rocket.

Only a few more rungs . . . Now three . . . Now two . . . Now only one . . . This is it!

This is it! . . . I've walked a few steps! . . . For the first time in the history of mankind there is an EXPLORER ON THE MOON!

But already I'm not alone . . . There's the Captain coming to join me.

On the Moon! . . . It's terrific! . . . I'm walking on the Moon! . . . I'm walking . . . running . . . jumping!

?
?

Good heavens, what a leap!

Ha! ha! ha! You see, Captain! On the Moon, gravity is actually six times less than on Earth.
And I knew that all the time, thundering typhoons! . . . But I'd completely forgotten.

There! Look at the Earth! . . . Our good old Earth. It looks four times bigger than the Moon does, when we see it at home.
Let's hope we'll be able to get back there one day!

Hello Tintin . . . Here's Snowy coming to join you. I'll follow him down.
WOOAAAH! . . .

You see. There was no need to get so excited.
That's what you think!

Anyway, I'm not sorry to have a chance to stretch my legs!

Golly! now I've taken off like a dragon-fly!

The Moon! . . . Just imagine, walking calmly along on the Moon! . . . Old Calculus is an incredible fellow!

?
?

What happened? . . .
Was that an earthquake?
A Moon-quake, more likely, but . . .

Great snakes! . . . Look there!
Thundering typhoons! What in the world's that? . . .

A meteorite! Look, a meteorite! It's just fallen on the exact spot where we were a moment ago . . . and exploded!
Exploded? But I didn't hear a sound!

Naturally not. There's no air on the Moon, so there's no noise . . . And that's why the meteorite came down intact, too. Back at home, on the Earth, the friction of the atmosphere would have made it white hot. So it would have disintegrated before reaching the ground, making what we generally call a "shooting star".

Anyway, if those tycoons on the lunar development corporation imagine that this sort of welcome will attract tourists to the Moon, they'll have to think again.

Ah, hello my friends! . . . This is incredible! . . . It's fantastic! . . . We're on the Moon! D'you realise that?
Oh, so there you are!

Just take a look there! . . . A little bit closer, and you'd have been able to throw away our return tickets!
A meteorite! How marvellous!

Oh, so you think that's marvellous, do you? When we'd have been as flat as pancakes!
What do you expect? It's an occupational hazard!

Exactly, blistering barnacles! But this isn't my occupation! Thundering typhoons, I'm a sailor! . . . And on board ship, at least you don't run the risk of bits of sky falling down all over the place, every time you bat an eyelid!
Maybe! . . . But just try coming to the Moon by boat!

Still, that's not the point. We must set to work. Come along and unload the cargo. We must start at once. Wolff has already got everything prepared.

But I wonder what he's waiting for . . . Hello, Wolff . . . This is Calculus calling. Can you hear me, Wolff? . . . Hello?

Good heavens, what's happening? . . . The ladder . . . The door . . . Captain, look!

The ladder's retracted! . . . The door is shut! . . . What in the world does this mean?
Hello, Wolff?

Hello, Wolff, hello? Blistering barnacles, what are you playing at up there? Hello, hello! . . . Hello Wolff? Thundering typhoons, are you going to answer me?

Hello? Hello? . . . Ah, there's the ladder again. And the door has been reopened.

You certainly gave us a fright, Wolff! . . . We thought for a moment that the rocket was suddenly going to take off and return to Earth, leaving us stuck here in this delightful place!

I'm terribly sorry . . . I . . . Just a mistake . . . So stupid . . . I wasn't thinking . . .

Never mind, forget about it! . . . Now Wolff, we're going to discharge the cargo. The Captain's coming up to help you get the crates out of the holds. Tintin and I will stay down here.

It's quite a simple job. Each crate is bound with steel wires connected to a central ring. You only have to slip the ring over the hook on the pulley-block.
Right! . . . I'll go up and join Wolff.

Moon-Rocket to Earth . . . Calculus calling . . . We've just been discharging the cargo. Everything is going very smoothly.

The hours go by . . .

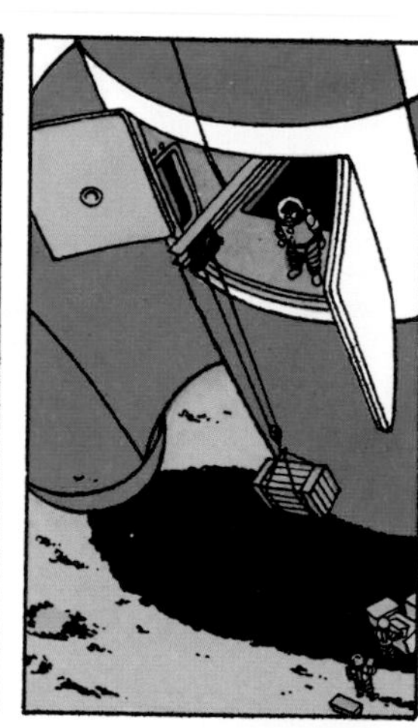

There . . . As far as the cargo's concerned, we'll soon have finished. But we've still got to unload the reconnaissance tank.

Hello, Captain? Next one please.

!!!

?
. . . heavens! Mind out!

A-2

Young man, would you be kind enough to explain the meaning of this ridiculous prank?

Billions of blue blistering barnacles! I'd thank Tintin if I were you. Without him you'd have been smashed to pulp!

Look, Professor. Was I wrong to push you over?

The wires have parted. Just look there; they've been worn through by friction. It must have been caused by the vibrations to the rocket towards the end of the journey.

We certainly had a bit of luck! Shall we carry on, Captain? But this time be sure to check the wires.

And how! I'll make doubly sure!

I say, Wolff, we're going to carry on . . . By Christopher, Wolff, what's the matter?

I . . . I don't know . . . I felt dizzy . . . suddenly . . . I thought I was going to faint. Perhaps it's my heart . . . I . . . It'll go: I feel better already.

Don't worry, Wolff; probably it's only fatigue. And perhaps your oxygen supply is badly adjusted. Go and lie down. In fact, we'll all follow suit.

A few minutes later . . .
Moon-Rocket to Earth. We've just come back on board for a bit of a rest. Meanwhile the two detectives have gone out to have a turn at exploring.

Imagine! Here we are, strolling on the surface of the Moon, where the hand of man has never set foot!
Hm! . . . Really never?

Stop, my dear fellow! Stop!

A crevasse! By jove, we must watch our step!

For goodness' sake be careful!

!
?

Did you see that? It's amazing! A standing jump, too!

It's your turn now. Come on, don't be scared!

What d'you think of that, eh? Even further than you, old man!

I've had an idea. Hold my hand. We're going to dance a little ballet!
A ballet? . . . All right, if you want to . . .

Ha! ha! ha!
Ha! ha! ha!

Ha ha ha! ha ha ha!
Come on, be serious! Supposing people saw us!

People! . . . Ha! ha! . . . PEOPLE!
Well why not?

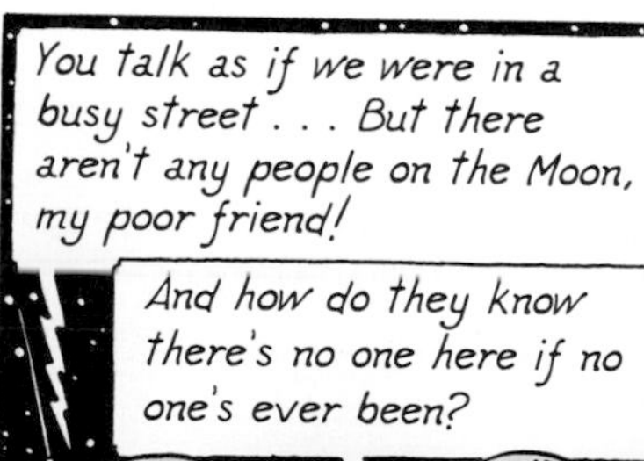
You talk as if we were in a busy street . . . But there aren't any people on the Moon, my poor friend!

And how do they know there's no one here if no one's ever been?

?
Besides, look there!

Well? . . . You see? What did I tell you?
Footsteps! . . . There's someone else besides us on the Moon!

Hello, this is Thompson . . . with a 'p' as in Percival . . . Calling Moon-Rocket . . .
Moon-Rocket here . . . Calculus speaking. We are receiving you.

Thompson calling . . . We've made a sensational discovery . . . Sen-sa-tion-al, d'you hear? Listen to this: there are people on the Moon!
What sort of fairy-tale is that! People? Other people? . . . Nonsense!

But there are! We've discovered footsteps!
Footsteps? But great sunspots, they're obviously footsteps made by one of us.

They can't be made by ONE of us: there are TWO sets of footsteps!
Quite right!

Then they're footsteps made by two of us, nitwit! . . . I expect you've gone back on your tracks, and those are your own footmarks!

Great Scotland Yard! Have we been going round in circles, following our own tracks - as in the desert?
Definitely not! Because there are two sets of tracks, and we're alone!

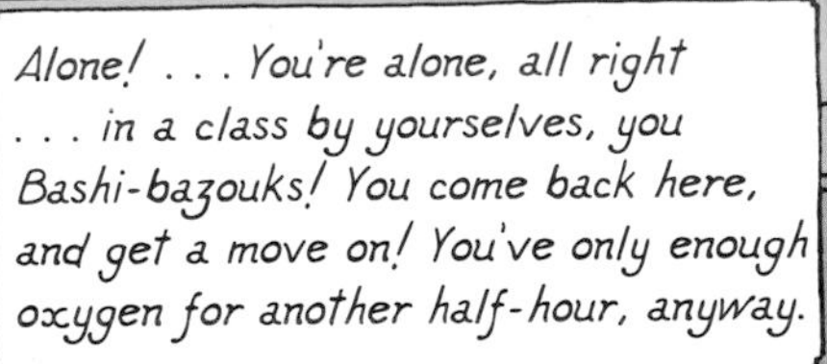
Alone! . . . You're alone, all right . . . in a class by yourselves, you Bashi-bazouks! You come back here, and get a move on! You've only enough oxygen for another half-hour, anyway.

All right, all right, we're coming . . . Since you despise our scientific contributions . . .

Perhaps it's silly, but I wonder . . . Those footsteps they saw . . . What if there are other men on the Moon? D'you think that's absolutely impossible?

Impossible? . . . Theoretically, no. If we were able to get here, then others could too. But as far as I'm concerned, I'm certain we are the first - and the only people - to land on the Moon.
Oh, good.

They can say what they like in there . . . We'll see who's right in the end.
Yes, yes . . . Patience!

A few minutes later . . .

Gentlemen, our plan was to stay on the Moon for a whole lunar day – that's equivalent to fourteen terrestrial days. But our oxygen supplies were intended for four people and one dog, and not for six people, which is our present number. So we shall have to restrict our stay to six days.

We must therefore hasten our work. While Wolff and I set up our observational instruments, Tintin and the Captain will unload the components of our reconnaissance tank and assemble it. Is that agreed? Right then, gentlemen, let's get to work!

EXTRACT FROM THE LOG BOOK BY PROFESSOR CALCULUS

3rd June – 2345 hrs. (G.M.T.). Unloading of cargo completed. Wolff and I have started to install the observatory. Ceased work at 2200 hrs. Captain Haddock and Tintin have begun assembling the tank.

4th June – 0830 hrs. Operations commenced at 0400 hrs (G.M.T.). Telescope mounted: Cameras in position. Theodolite in working order.

Moon to Earth . . . Calculus calling . . . The optical instruments and cameras are ready for use. We are beginning our observational work.

Observe away, my friends. You do that! Your discoveries will be vastly interesting . . . TO US! Ha! ha! ha! ha!

EXTRACT FROM THE LOG BOOK BY PROFESSOR CALCULUS

4th June – 2150 hrs. (G.M.T.). Wolff and I spent the day studying cosmic rays, and making astronomical observations. Our findings have been entered progressively in Special Record Books Nos. I and II. The Captain and Tintin have nearly finished assembling the tank.

5th. June – 1920 hrs. (G.M.T.). Half an hour ago the Captain and Tintin pronounced the tank ready for use.

Moon to Earth . . . Calculus calling . . . The tank is ready. We're going to make the first trials. Tintin will be in charge. He's just entering the turret.

He has just secured the hatch. Now they are filling the insulated cabin with air. When this is done they can remove their space-suits; then Tintin will take the controls and the Captain will act as lookout.

Ah, there's Tintin's head showing through the multiplex cockpit cover. He's smiling at me and signalling that everything's in order.

And there's the Captain. Like Tintin, he's signalling to us that all's well. He's wearing his head-phones and . . .

Hello, Haddock calling . . . Ready for departure . . . Hello there, Tintin, weigh the anchor!
OK . . . Off we go!
Good luck!

!

Billions of blue blistering barnacles, Tintin! Couldn't you cast off more smoothly?

I'm sorry. It's the first time I've driven this sort of machine . . .

. . . but don't you think I've learnt a lot already?

Hey, Tintin! This is a tank you're driving, not a thundering motor-scooter! . . . We're on the Moon, you know, not in a Fun-Fair!
I'm doing my best, but . . .

Steady! Hang on tight!

Tintin calling . . . Apart from the bumps, everything's fine.

You won't catch me being a regular passenger in your blistering taxi!

HELP!

Stop, Tintin, for heaven's sake! Stop! . . . This is ghastly! My microphone's bust . . . Tintin can't hear me!

Great snakes! A crevasse! . . . Stop!

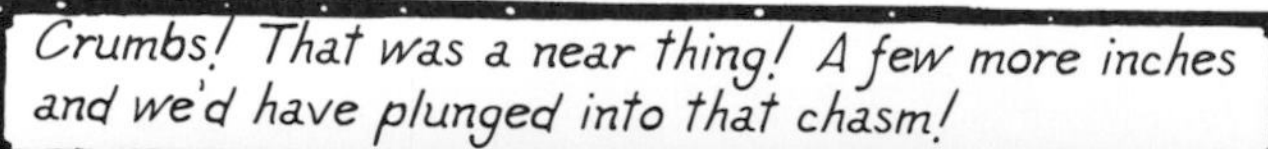

Crumbs! That was a near thing! A few more inches and we'd have plunged into that chasm!

Blistering barnacles, it's a mere detail that I cracked my head against that cover again! . . . But we've had enough! We're going home! We know now that the tank goes well . . . and that crash helmets are indispensable!
I agree. I'll reverse, and we'll go back to Base.

EXTRACT FROM THE LOG BOOK
BY PROFESSOR CALCULUS

*6th June - 1340 hrs. (G.M.T.)
This is a day that will go down in the annals of Science. We have succeeded in making direct measurement of the constant of solar radiation, and fixing exactly the limits of the solar spectrum in the ultra-violet. An hour ago, at 1235 precisely, Wolff, the Captain, Tintin and Snowy set off on a reconnaissance trip in the tank, towards the crater Ptolemaeus.*

Tank calling Base. All's going well on board.

Whew! It's hot under this flower-pot! I'm positively melting!

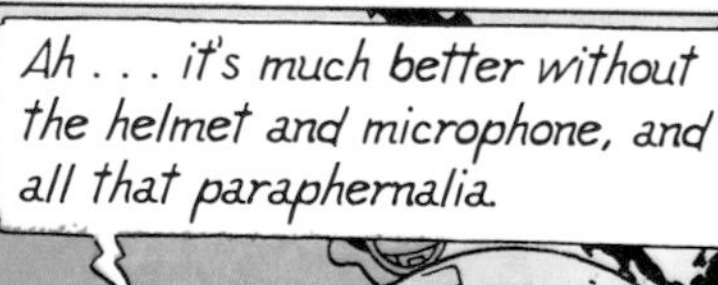

Ah . . . it's much better without the helmet and microphone, and all that paraphernalia.

I say! . . . What's that I can see over there?

STOP!

Right, I'm drawing up.

Look there, over on your left: at the foot of the cliff!
?
?

See down there, behind that finger of rock . . .
It looks like the entrance to a cave.

That's just what I thought. We'd better have a closer look at it.
Right, I'll go across. Are you coming too, Captain?
OK, I'm with you.

Hello, Wolff . . . You're quite right. It's definitely the entrance to a cave.

It remains to be seen where it leads to. Come on. I'll switch on my lamp.

Blistering barnacles! I've done a good many things in my time . . . but never lunar spelaeology!

We're in a proper cathedral!

Stalagmites and stalactites . . . This proves that at some period there was water on the Moon.

Snowy, Snowy, don't go far ahead. Be careful, and stay close to us.
He doesn't seem to realise that I'm grown up! Honestly! What does he take me for? Granny's little lap-dog?

WOOOAH!
!

Great snakes! A crevasse! He must have fallen in!

Quick, Captain. Hold tight! I'll try and shine a light down.

The crevasse bends sharply. I can't see far. Snowy! Snowy!

Quickly, Captain! Undo your rope and secure it to a rock.
But you aren't really going to . . .

Yes, yes. We must do all we can to try and save poor Snowy. Hurry! Tie me an absolutely firm knot.
There . . . But it's sheer madness . . .

All right?
All right?

For heaven's sake, Tintin, be careful! You know what it'll mean if you smash your oxygen pipe.
Yes. I know.
Ah! I'm standing on a sort of ledge . . . Snowy! Snowy!

Tintin, be sensible: come back! It's quite useless. You don't really imagine he could have survived a fall like that? . . . You must come back!
No, I'm going on. Perhaps he's only hurt.

The crevasse is widening. I'm still going down.

Oh! The rope is too short. I've come to the end. I can't go down any further.

You see, you donkey! Blistering barnacles, come on up!

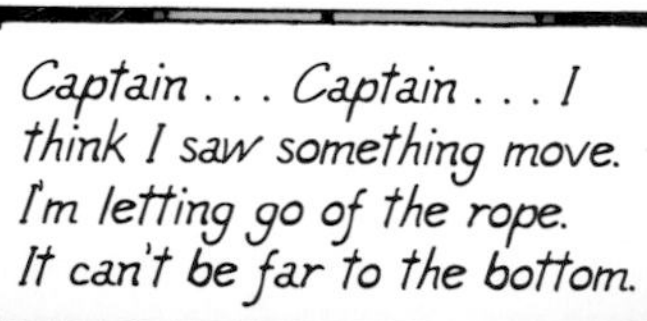

Captain . . . Captain . . . I think I saw something move. I'm letting go of the rope. It can't be far to the bottom.

You're crazy! Tintin, don't do that!

Into the hands of Fate!

You're right. I'll come up . . . Snowy! . . . Snowy!

Great snakes! . . . Ice!

Snowy! . . . You're there! Nothing broken? But what's the matter? You aren't answering . . . Oh, now I see: your radio isn't working.

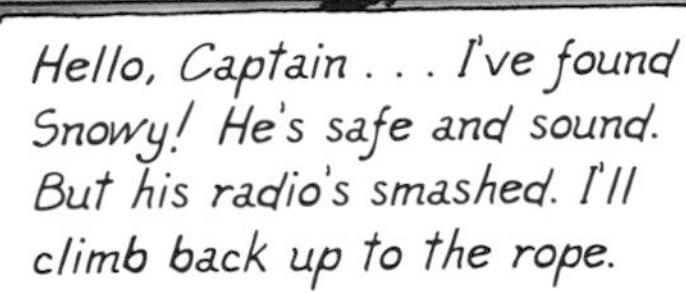
Hello, Captain . . . I've found Snowy! He's safe and sound. But his radio's smashed. I'll climb back up to the rope.

My dear Tintin, you don't imagine you can stand up on this skating-rink, do you?

You see? What did I tell you?

Crumbs! How can I climb this icy slope? . . . There's only one way to do it: by cutting steps with a chunk of rock. Oh well, to work!

Hello, Captain . . . Untie the rope and let it down as far as possible . . . When I manage to reach it I'll tie Snowy on, and you can pull him up . . . Then I'll follow.
OK.

Here we are at last!

Hello, Captain. Let out more rope: it isn't down far enough for me to tie it round Snowy.
Right.

That's done it.

A few minutes later . . .
Hello Tintin . . . That's it . . . Snowy is safe now.
?

Hello Tintin . . . I've secured a heavy stone to the end of the rope. I'm letting it down . . .

All right, Captain. But hurry: it's beginning to get difficult to breathe.

I'm almost at the end. Can you see the rope?

No, I can't see it. Do please hurry!

Blistering barnacles, what's up? The rope's somehow got shorter than it was just now.

Oh! . . . I can't feel the weight of the stone any longer . . . It must have come off, or else it's wedged somewhere. Quick, start again . . .

Meanwhile . . .
Hello, Wolff . . . Well, what news?

Wolff here . . . Still no sign. It's more than half an hour since they went into the cave. I'm beginning to wonder if . . . Ah, there they are!

Heavens! Tintin's staggering - he looks pretty groggy. The Captain's almost carrying him. Hello, Captain, is he hurt?

No. But he's just about reached the end of his tether, poor lad.

Saved! My friends, they're saved!

Tank calling Base. The Captain and Tintin are back on board. The Captain's taken over command as Tintin is completely exhausted. We're returning post-haste!

Some hours later . . .
Moon-Rocket to Earth . . . Calculus calling. The tank is back, but is going off at once. This time the Captain, Thomson and Thompson, and myself will be on board. Our trip will last about forty-eight hours. Our aim is to do a more careful survey of the caves discovered by Tintin; they may contain rich deposits of uranium, or radium.

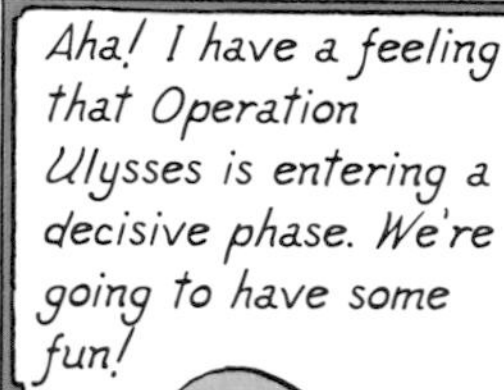
Aha! I have a feeling that Operation Ulysses is entering a decisive phase. We're going to have some fun!

A few minutes later . . .
Tank calling Base. We're leaving now. Goodbye!

Moon-Rocket calling . . . Tintin here. Good luck and good hunting! . . . And don't leave us alone for too long!

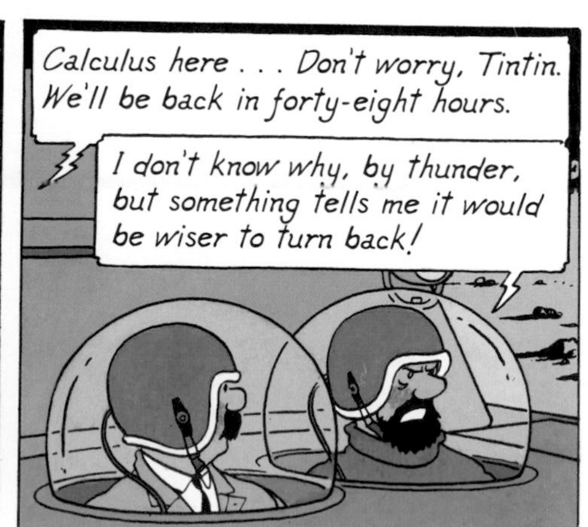
Calculus here . . . Don't worry, Tintin. We'll be back in forty-eight hours.
I don't know why, by thunder, but something tells me it would be wiser to turn back!

Goodbye . . . See you soon. I'm going to start mending the radios on our space-suits. Goodbye!

Goodbye, Tintin! . . . Goodbye, Wolff!

It's time for a meal. I . . . er . . . I'll go down to the stores to find something for lunch . . .
A good idea, too. I'm dog tired of waiting.

Would you like me to go?
No, no . . . er . . . don't you bother. I'll go myself.

It's strange how Wolff has altered. At first, in the centre at Sprodj, he was smiling and happy . . . He's not the same man at all now. What can have changed him so?
I never cared for him much. And I've got a good nose!

A few minutes later . . .
There . . . I've found all we need.
If only it were a tin of bones!

Oh, bother!
Why, what's the matter?
?

Er . . . nothing much. I forgot to bring any tinned milk . . . I'll have to go down to the stores again.

Certainly not. This time it's my turn to go.
Oh, all right. Thank you. It's very kind of you.

You'll see the box right in front of you as you go in.
Good.

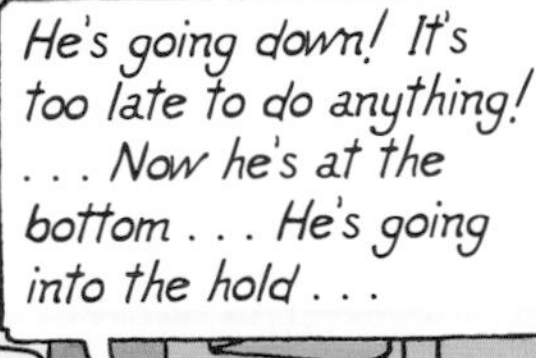
He's going down! It's too late to do anything! . . . Now he's at the bottom . . . He's going into the hold . . .

Aha, my young friend. You never expected that one day Colonel Jorgen would come as far as the Moon for his revenge, did you?
24

Wolff! Hi, Wolff! I've done it. You can come . . .

I . . . I'm coming.

Good heavens . . . you . . . you haven't . . . after all . . . too hard?

No, no, don't worry. I've just . . . put him to sleep! And now, Wolff, back we go to Earth.
What? . . . What do you mean? Without waiting for the others?

Without waiting for the others - of course! Tell me: how soon can the rocket be ready for take-off?
No, we can't do that! . . . Marooning them on the Moon will condemn them to a hideous death. It would be an atrocious crime!

Tut-tut! Cut out the fine words, my dear Wolff! And cut out the noble sentiments, too! We're leaving, and that's that!
No! I refuse to do it! I won't be a party to such a monstrous deed!

My dear Wolff, listen to me! Supposing we wait for the others to come back, and overpower them one by one as they leave the air-lock. Right . . . Then, we set off for the Earth with our prisoners . . . But the oxygen . . . what about the oxygen, eh Wolff?

Supplies were provided for four people: we are seven. So? It's too easy: we'll all be dead before the end of the journey. Is that what you want? . . . Well? Answer me! . . . Good . . . Now you're seeing sense! . . . Come with me. We'll go up and prepare for departure.

Ah, here's Tintin coming up again.

!
?

Wooah! . . . Wooah! . . . Grrr . . . Bang! . . . Thump!

Hello, Tintin . . . Tank calling . . . What's all that hullabaloo?

Hello, Wolff here . . . I . . . er . . . It's nothing . . . Tintin went below . . . and Snowy, you see . . . Snowy wanted to follow him. But it's all over now . . .

How right you are! It's over for good!

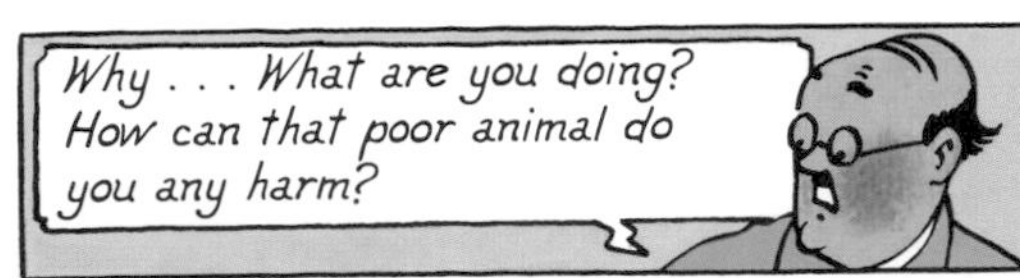
Why . . . What are you doing? How can that poor animal do you any harm?

You never can tell, Wolff! This wretched mongrel could make trouble for us later on.

So that's that! And now, my friend, you're going to cook me a nice hot meal. For eight days I've been living on dry sandwiches, and I've had enough of them! So get moving! . . . And don't waste any time!

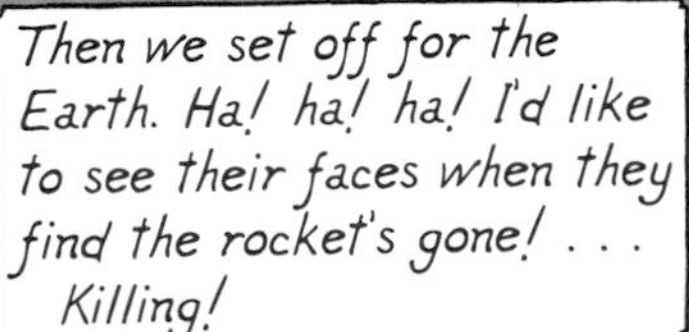
Then we set off for the Earth. Ha! ha! ha! I'd like to see their faces when they find the rocket's gone! . . . Killing!

Is that food coming, Wolff? I'm as hungry as a lion!

In a minute . . . I . . . Not long now . . .

Hello! Tank calling Base!
?

We've had a breakdown. The motor batteries are flat. A short-circuit, I expect. The Captain is just connecting the small emergency batteries, so that we can get back to Base.

By Lucifer! They're coming back! We must take off immediately! Leave your pots and pans, Wolff . . . We're on our way, at once!

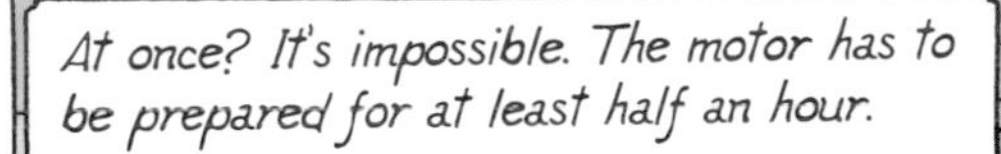
At once? It's impossible. The motor has to be prepared for at least half an hour.

Fool! Couldn't you have remembered that sooner? Well, hurry! What are you waiting for?

Meanwhile . . .

Crumbs, what am I doing here? . . . And . . . Oooh my head! . . . But what . . . I'm tied up!! . . . What's happened to me?
24

I don't understand at all. I . . . Why, what's that humming noise? Good heavens! It's the motor . . . But then . . . then . . . the rocket's going to take off . . .
24

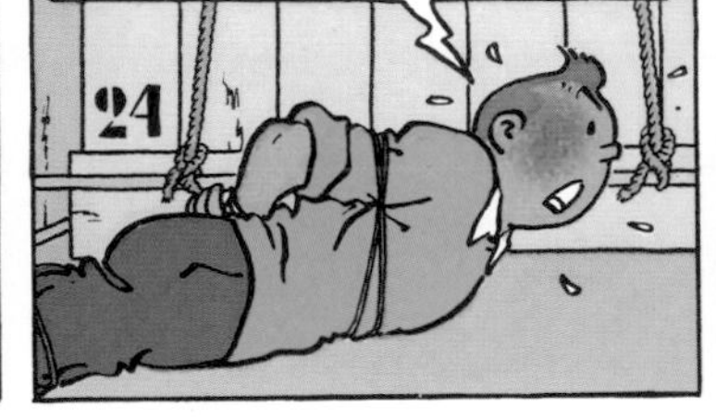
But where are the others? Prisoners like myself? But come to think of it . . . Poor devils! They went off in the tank . . . Are they going to be left on the Moon? Wolff! Wolff! HELP!
24

Tank calling Base . . . We're returning at reduced speed. We can see the rocket . . . Can you hear me? . . .

Ready yet?

Another quarter of an hour.

This is Tank calling Moon-Rocket . . . Are you receiving me? Answer please.

How odd. The ladder has retracted. And the door is closed. What can be the meaning of that?

Well Wolff? Can we go?
No, not yet.

It will take ten minutes. If I press now, we shan't take off. You have to wait till the red light goes on in the centre of the panel.

Tank calling Moon-Rocket. We're nearly home. Let down the ladder and open the doors. Hello, Moon-Rocket . . .

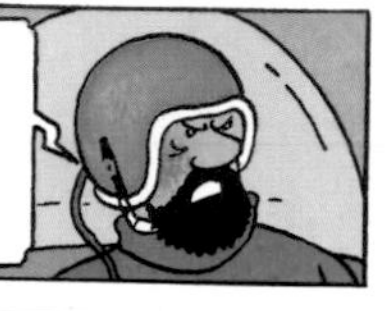
I tell you, there's something fishy going on inside that thundering rocket!

Aren't you ready yet?

Nearly . . . only another three minutes.

Moon-Rocket, Moon-Rocket! What are you playing at? Answer me!

This is Tank calling Moon-Rocket . . . Tank calling Moon-Rocket . . . Can you hear me?
Stand by . . . Get ready . . . I'm going to press the button!

?
!
!

What the devil . . . The rocket! . . . Look . . . It's going . . .

No . . . it's fallen back . . . The engine has stopped!

?
?

Great sunspots! The rocket's off balance . . . It's swaying . . . It's going to fall on its side!

No, thank goodness! It's still upright! . . . But what lunatic suddenly decided to set off the launching mechanism?

Confound it! We're back on the ground. What's happened, Wolff?

I . . . I don't understand. We began to rise normally . . . then the engine simply stopped. There's no reason at all . . .

Where's the prize nincompoop who pulled this half-witted stunt? Blistering barnacles, I've got a thing or two to say to him! . . .

Ah, it just occurs to me, Wolff . . . You and your conscientious scruples . . . If you've sabotaged the launching gear, I swear you'll pay dearly for it!

Me? Sabotaged it? How could I have done? W-what are you doing? . . . NO! . . . NO!

Listen to me, Wolff. I'll count up to ten. If we're not safely on our way by the time I get to ten, I'll put a bullet through your brains!

Hello, Tintin . . . Wolff? Come on, why don't you answer? Thundering typhoons, open up!

Four . . . five . . . six . . .
Mercy! I beg of you! Mercy!

Seven . . . eight . . . nine . . .

And ten! The rocket's not moved. You asked for it, Wolff! I'll fire . . .

AAAAHH!

TINTIN!

Yes, me! . . . Did I disturb you? I do beg your pardon. I really should have knocked before I came in. Now get up, both of you, and put up your hands!

It's a small world, isn't it, Colonel Boris? . . . You haven't changed much since the days when you plotted against your master, the King of Syldavia.

By the way, you accused poor Wolff of having sabotaged the launching gear. I'm sorry to disillusion you: I was the culprit.

Tintin, Tintin, where are you?
Here, Captain. Come up quickly!

Billions of blue blistering barnacles! Where did this jack-pudding come from? Off the Moon?

No, out of the hold, where he was hiding - thanks to the treachery of our friend Wolff. Will you get busy tying them up, while we're waiting for the others?

Ah, there you are at last, Professor Calculus. Do come in. This gentleman is so anxious to make your acquaintance.
Who are you, sir? And what are you doing here?
So you prevented me from smoking my poor little pipe, Wolff, just to let this thundering Bashi-Bazouk have his ration of oxygen?

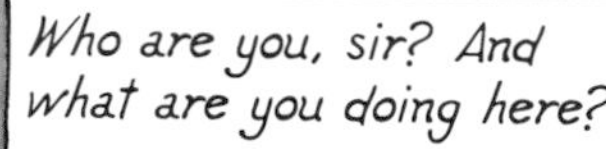

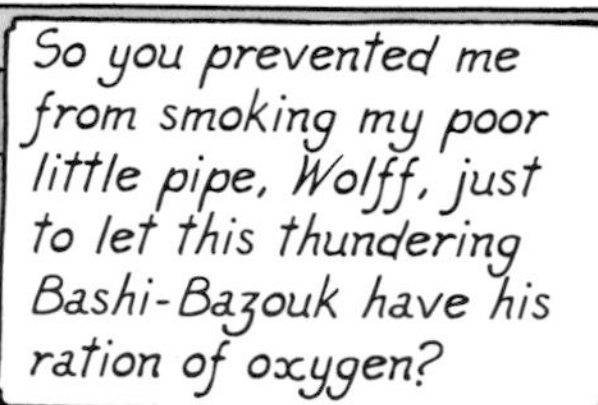

You may as well know at once that it's a waste of time questioning me. I'm not talking! You'd better interrogate Wolff: he'll be only too happy to spill the beans, the wood-louse!

In heaven's name, Wolff, what's the meaning of this? What's going on? . . . I can't make it out . . . It's all a misunderstanding, isn't it? . . . Come along, Wolff, tell me. Explain yourself.
I'm ashamed . . . So utterly ashamed . . .

Tintin! . . . Tintin! . . . Quick!
?

Quick, quick! I think Snowy's leg is broken!
What? I'm coming at once.

I'm afraid you're right. I saw him lying unconscious a few minutes ago. But there was other urgent work to be done. I'll carry him up to the cabin.

Well?
Yes, his leg's broken.

You hear that, you unfeeling monsters? . . . Vivisectionists! . . . Torturers! . . . Cannibals!

Anyway, who says that his leg's broken? Wait a minute; I'm going to have a look at it for myself.

Now then, Snowy boy. Captain Haddock's going to examine you . . . There . . . Let's see your paw . . . Does that hurt? No, not at all, eh?

!?
WOOAAAH

I . . . er . . . you see: I have a way with animals . . . It's one of my strong points. But I wonder if it wouldn't be better . . .

A few minutes later . . .
There we are, Snowy. A few days' rest, and you'll be fine.

Now then, back to these gentlemen. We're waiting for your explanation, Wolff.

Yes . . . I'll tell you everything.

Three years ago I was working in America at the rocket proving ground at White Sands. None of this would have occurred if I'd not had a passion for gambling . . . I got into debt . . . Then one day, in New York, a man approached me. He said he knew my situation, and was ready to settle my debts in exchange for a little harmless information . . .

. . . about the nuclear research I was engaged on. But little by little he put pressure on me to reveal real secrets. At first, I refused. But my creditors were hounding me. I was trapped . . . Finally I gave in . . . A spy - that's what I had become. But one day I rebelled. I wanted to become an honest man again, and I fled to Europe . . . In the end I came to Syldavia, where I heard they were building an atomic centre. I got a job there.

When you arrived in Sprodj I was happy, and had forgotten the whole business. Then one day I received a message. They had picked up my trail; they ordered me to furnish them with complete details of the experimental rocket we were just finishing. Otherwise my past would be revealed. Heartstricken, I surrendered.

So it was you who betrayed all the plans, and all the radio-control data!
It was I; yes, it was I.

Then it was you who nearly stove my head in, too, when I was lying in wait in the corridor at the Centre. Well, you'll pay for that all right!

One moment, Captain. We too have a question to ask the prisoner.
Yes, a vital question!

What about the skeleton, Wolff? Was that you?
Yes, skeleton, were you the Wolff? Come on, answer up!

Blistering barnacles, this is a SERIOUS interrogation! In other words, anacoluthons, you keep out of it!

All right, Wolff. Go on.

Well, thanks to Tintin, your enemies didn't succeed in capturing the trial rocket: you blew it up in flight. But they believed that it was I who betrayed them, and they threatened to kill me. Then they learned that this rocket was under construction, and they gave me fresh orders . . . One of the crates coming from Oberköchen would be faked, and would conceal a journalist. My part would be simply to facilitate his task . . .

And you believed a fairy-tale like that? You two-faced traitor! A cock-and-bull story! It would make a cat laugh!
Er . . . they said he'd reveal his presence once the rocket reached the Moon.

Then, soon after our arrival here, I took advantage of your absence to let him out of his hiding place. It was Jorgen. He divulged his real objective: to capture the rocket and take it back, not to Sprodj, but to the country for which he works.

Two more points, Wolff . . . The ladder being retracted . . . and the crate that nearly squashed us: was that you?
Yes! . . . And when you were just behind me pretending to have an attack of dizziness, you meant to push me out into space, eh, gangster?

And I trusted you implicitly . . . Oh! Wolff! . . .
Well, go on.
Yes, out with it, Judas!

Today, when Tintin was alone on board and the rest of you had departed for forty-eight hours, the Colonel decided to act. At the given moment, Tintin went down into the hold . . .
That's to say, you'd been first, to set your accomplice free. Then you managed to arrange that I'd go down myself.

Er . . . yes . . . I stayed here, and it was he who knocked out Tintin. It was only afterwards that he told me of his plan to abandon you on the Moon. I tried to stop him . . . I swear I did!

I believe you. This is what happened then . . . When I came round I was in the hold, trussed up like a chicken . . . I heard the humming of the motor, and realised what was going on . . . Luckily for us, these two worthy characters were never Boy Scouts!

I mean that they don't know how to tie a knot! So I managed to get rid of my ropes without too much difficulty. And none too soon! The engine was just starting. As the rocket was rising, I severed all the leads. The motor stopped immediately, and the rocket fell back to the ground . . .
And thanks to Tintin, we were saved!

Saved? . . . Ah, my poor friends, I only hope that you are not rejoicing too soon!

Undoubtedly by cutting the leads Tintin averted disaster . . . for the time being. Alas, it is only too likely that in falling, the rocket suffered serious damage. And this will probably take time to repair. Meanwhile, there's still the grave problem of the oxygen . . . But let's hear the rest of your story, Tintin.

Where was I? . . . Oh yes. Once the rocket grounded, I opened the door of the air-lock and lowered the retractable ladder, so that you could get in. Then, having armed myself with a pistol and spanner, I came quietly up to the cabin . . . I found myself right in the middle of a family squabble . . .

This thug accused Wolff of sabotaging the launching gear, and was going to shoot him. My spanner knocked his gun out of his hand. Just in time, wasn't it, my dear Jorgen . . . as it seems that you are no longer Colonel Boris.
Why, do you know this pithecanthropus?

Oh yes, we met in Syldavia, over that business of King Ottokar's Sceptre. Under the name of Boris, he was aide-de-camp to King Muskar XII, whom he shamefully betrayed. I won the first round, but for a while he seemed to be winning the second . . .

And now we'll dump these two down in the hold.
What? . . . While we risk running out of oxygen, we're going to clutter the place up with these pirates? They were going to abandon us on the Moon: well, that's the fate they deserve themselves, by thunder!

We must be more chivalrous than they were, Captain . . . Now, you're the expert, so take them below and tie them up securely.

As you like! But you'll live to regret your noble gesture. Mark my words: you'll regret it!

Anyway, my little lambs, I'm going to knit you lovely little rope waistcoats to keep you nice and warm! Hand-made, by thunder! Guaranteed absolutely perfect!

Do what you like with me. But please be kind enough to stop spluttering in my face – it's wet!
!

What? . . . Me? . . . Wet? . . . Blistering barnacles, you dare . . . A man of spirit like me! To hear myself insulted, by this creature, this Bashi-bazouk!
Calm down, Captain, calm down!

Calm down? Calm down? . . . But you heard him, this little black-beetle! Daring to make out that I'm wet! Calm down! I like that, from you!

To call me wet! . . . What a nerve!

Calculus has got one.
Yes, I'll fetch it.

!?

Come now, Captain, the incident is closed. Go on down to the hold with the two prisoners.
That's right. In the meantime I'll get in touch with the Earth and tell them what's been happening.

Moon-Rocket calling Earth. There have been extremely serious developments here . . . A traitor, in the service of some unknown Power, was secretly smuggled aboard the rocket.

. . . Wolff was his accomplice . . . Yes, Wolff! . . . Today they went into action and tried to seize control of the rocket. Fortunately we have managed to overpower them, and put a stop to their mischief . . .

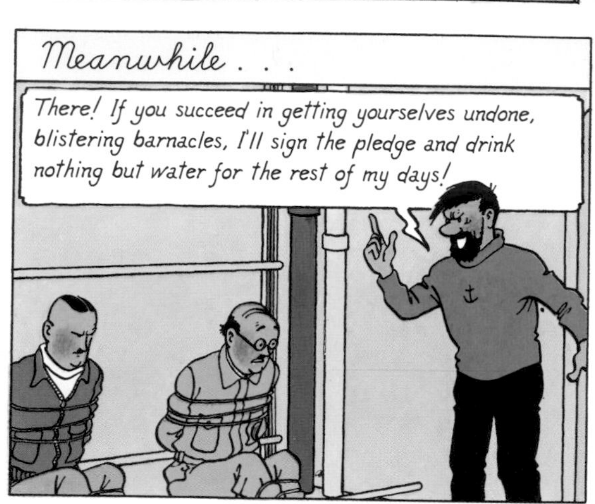

Meanwhile . . .
There! If you succeed in getting yourselves undone, blistering barnacles, I'll sign the pledge and drink nothing but water for the rest of my days!

A few minutes later . . .
That's done! Our two chump chops are now on ice!
Good. Now for my news . . .

I've just made a superficial inspection of the damage to the rocket. My preliminary estimate is that it will take us at least a hundred hours to effect the necessary repairs.

To that must be added the time for our return journey. We have oxygen supplies for a hundred hours at the most, which means that having used our last resources to re-launch the rocket, we shall run the risk of arriving on Earth as corpses.

Perhaps! But meanwhile we're still very much alive. And we'll start work at once. At all costs we must get everything finished in the shortest possible time!

Moon-Rocket to Earth. We're going to begin the repair work. Give us some music: it will keep up our morale.

Earth to Moon-Rocket. We'll switch on Radio-Klow for you. Keep your spirits up!

Come on, come on, cry-babies! To work! And none of those gloomy thoughts. We're going to have some music. Thundering typhoons, there's nothing like a bit of music to cheer you up!

This is Radio-Klow. Our programme continues with "The Gravedigger", by Schubert.

The time passes . . . Slowly, the lunar night falls on the desolate landscape . . .

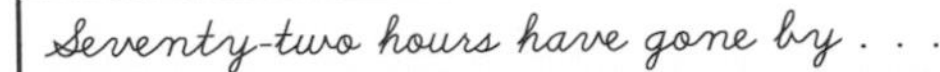
Seventy-two hours have gone by . . .

Moon-Rocket to Earth . . . The work is well ahead. Barring accidents, we shall have finished by midday . . . However, we are having to abandon the tank and the optical instruments on the Moon. To dismantle them and then reload them would take too long, in view of the little oxygen remaining.

We are only keeping the recording instruments, the cameras, and, of course, the oxygen cylinders from the tank. They constitute our final reserves. Tintin and the Captain have gone to collect them. I'm switching over now, as I want to keep in touch with them.
Right.

Hello Tintin . . . Calculus here . . . How are you getting on?

All right, thanks. But the sun has completely vanished. Only the mountain-tops are still glowing on the horizon . . .

But it's not preventing us from seeing, as there's a wonderful light from the Earth.
Pom Pom Pom And they danced by the light of the Earth

We have left a message sealed inside the tank for those who may one day follow in our steps. If we are lost with all hands, this message will be a reminder of the fantastic adventures of the first men on the Moon. Now we are coming back on board.

A few minutes later . . .
Everything's in order, Professor.
Good. Well, I've finished all the repairs. Earth have just given me the result of their reckoning. Take-off should be at 16.52 hours. So we have about two hours to go.

I advise you to lie down, to save oxygen. But before doing that, Captain, would you go to the hold and make the prisoners lie down as well, so that they won't suffer too much.
What?? And would you like me to take them breakfast in bed?

Keeping them is crazy enough! But to coddle them like babes in arms . . . blistering barnacles, that's the limit! Still, I'll go.

Patience! I've not struck my last blow yet! But ssh! Someone's coming . . .

Two hours later . . .
Earth calling Moon-Rocket . . . Stand by . . . Stand by . . .

Thirty seconds to go . . . Twenty seconds to go . . . Ten seconds to go . . . nine . . . eight . . . seven . . . six . . . five . . . four . . . three . . . two . . . one . . . ZERO!

I press the button . . . and pray that everything works properly! Otherwise, we're condemned to death!

Success! . . . Wonderful! . . .
Marvellous! . . . We're off!

And just for a change, blistering barnacles, we're going to pass out!

And upon the shadowy world a few footsteps remain, the only trace of the first EXPLORERS ON THE MOON.

They're on their way! The only thing that matters now is that they should have enough oxygen . . . But whatever happens, everything must be prepared for landing.

Is that the landing site? Giovanni? . . . Baxter here . . . If all goes well, the rocket will be here later today. Make sure everything's ready for their arrival; fire engines, ambulances . . . And get some electric saws ready, too, in case they haven't the strength to open the doors themselves. That's all for the moment.

I say, Mr Baxter, there's something wrong! Look: the rocket is deviating from the correct line of flight. I wonder what's happening . . .

By Jupiter! You're right! Perhaps the steering gear was damaged by the fall . . . Or else their gyroscopes have been put out of order . . . It's imperative that they correct their course . . . Call them, Walter!

This is Earth calling Moon-Rocket . . . Earth calling Moon-Rocket . . . Are you receiving me? . . .

No reply! . . . And they're getting further and further away! The poor devils! They're going to their death!

Earth calling Moon-Rocket . . . Are you receiving me?

Earth calling Moon-Rocket . . . Are you receiving me? . . . Earth calling Moon-Rocket . . .

Earth calling Moon-Rocket . . .
Earth calling Moon-Rocket . . .

Oh, the poor devils! . . . So much oxygen, simply being wasted . . . Heaven knows, they have little enough to play with . . .
Ssh! . . . They're answering!

Moon-Rocket to Earth . . . This is Tintin calling . . . I have just regained consciousness.

Earth to Moon-Rocket . . . Correct your line of flight at once: you are completely off course.
Right!

Quickly, Professor! Hurry! Come to the control cabin. We are off course!

I say! Where are you rushing off to like that?

Hi! Wait for me! I'm coming! What's happening?

Goodness gracious! This is disastrous! We're heading towards Jupiter!

Obviously the steering gear is out of alignment . . . Ah! That's done it, thank goodness!

Moon-Rocket to Earth . . . The steering gear was jammed . . . We are getting back on the right course.

Earth to Moon-Rocket . . . Well done! You're doing fine now!

Good. We can go below. That was a near thing!

And now that traitor Wolff isn't here to be such a kill-joy, we'll just cheer ourselves up. Let's have a drink all round . . . Tintin? . . . Professor?
By the way, where have the two detectives gone?

!
?
!
I'm just in time to bring you news of them!

Come on, hands up! . . . That's right . . . The boot's on the other foot now, isn't it, gentlemen?! Congratulations: you have two brilliant colleagues behind those moustaches!

Ha! ha! ha! . . . When they came to check on our ropes, they decided that handcuffs would be more secure! . . . And I'm ready to bet they won't get them undone in a hurry!

But that's enough talk! Gentlemen: you know the position. There isn't enough oxygen to go round. There are too many of us here. You spared my life: but I'm not going to spare yours!

But . . . but . . . you gave me your word that they would come to no harm.
And you were silly enough to believe me! . . . Out of my way: let me finish them off!

No, Jorgen, no! . . . You shall not do it! . . . Never!
What's got into you? Let go of me!

Will you get out! . . . Let go! . . . Let go of that, you fool!
Hold him, Wolff!

BANG!

Earth to Moon-Rocket . . . What's happened? We heard something that sounded like a shot . . .

It's all over. Nothing we can do.

Moon-Rocket to Earth . . . Calculus here . . . I . . . terrible . . . Jorgen managed to free himself . . . He wanted to kill us . . . and Wolff intervened . . . There was a fight . . . Jorgen had a gun in his hand . . . and in the struggle it went off . . . Jorgen was shot right through the heart.

I . . . I didn't mean to . . . He did it . . . himself . . .
I know, Wolff. You needn't blame yourself for what has just happened . . . Here are your glasses . . . Come and take your place among us again: I trust you.

What!! This interplanetary-pirate! This fresh-water-spaceman! Let him go free! Then, at the first opportunity this snake can . . . can stab us in the back! Into the hold with him, blistering barnacles! Into the hold, and in irons!

But . . . I . . . What's . . . what's the matter with me?

I understand; carbon dioxide is accumulating . . . and when you work yourself up . . .
He's right, Captain. Do please keep calm!
You do as you like! But on your own head be it if we have trouble from this scorpion, Wolff! I disclaim all responsibility!

Don't worry, nothing will happen. I'll answer for him. Now, it will be better to lie on our bunks: in that way we'll save oxygen.
But first of all we must go and release the two detectives . . . And what shall we do about Jorgen's body? . . .
The only answer is to leave it in space.

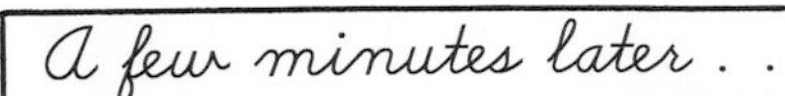
A few minutes later . . .

Earth to Moon-Rocket . . . Here is your latest position . . . You are now 31,000 miles from your point of departure . . . How are things going on board?

Moon-Rocket to Earth . . . The carbon dioxide is getting worse and worse . . . It's hard to breathe now . . . but still, for the moment, things are bearable . . .

The others are dozing on their bunks. I'm having to struggle to keep myself from falling asleep.

Earth to Moon-Rocket . . . Don't struggle, Tintin. Go to sleep. We'll wake you up when it's time for the turning operation.
Time goes by . . .
I think the coast is clear now. Everybody's asleep. This is my chance.

Let's hope no one wakes up! . . . No, all's well.

Where are you going, Wolff?

Ssh! Not so loud! . . . I'm going below, to the hold to . . . er . . . I think there's another cylinder of oxygen down there.
Oh, good.

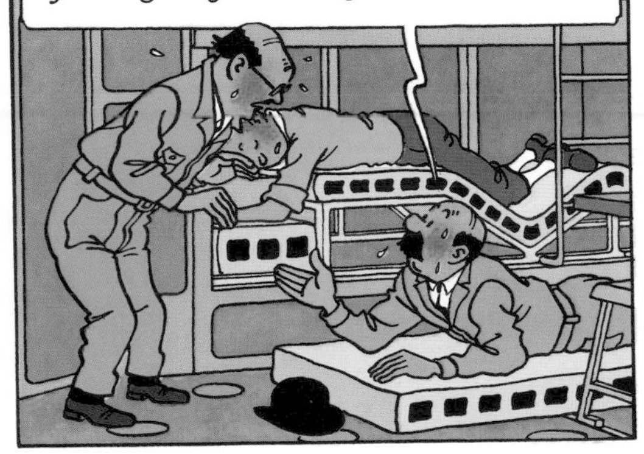
I had to ask, you see. The Captain particularly told me to give him details of every single move you made.

It's incredible . . . He hasn't given the alarm . . . Fate is on my side: I shall succeed!
Zzzz . . .
Zzzz . . .

Half an hour later . . .
Earth calling Moon-Rocket . . . Can you hear me? . . . Earth calling Moon-Rocket . . . Can you hear me? . . .

Can you hear me? . . . MOON-ROCKET!
What? . . . What's that? . . . Oh yes, the radio . . .

Moon-Rocket to Earth . . . Tintin here . . .
Ah! You really scared us!

Stand by . . . You have a quarter of an hour to go before the turning operation.
Right. We'll get ready. I'll wake up the others.

Wake up! . . . Everybody on the alert! Put on your magnetic-soled boots. In a quarter of an hour we have to turn the rocket round.
!

Ugh! More of those confounded acrobatics! I was just dreaming that I was by my fireside at Marlinspike with my cat on my knee . . . and instead . . .

WOLFF! . . . Blistering barnacles, where's Wolff? . . . His bunk's empty!

Don't worry, Captain. I know where Wolff is . . . He went down to the hold a few minutes ago.

And you let him go, you nitwitted nine-pin, you? . . . Even when I'd told you to keep an eye on him?
I did keep an eye on him; he told me himself he was going to the hold.

And you were so keen to play the big-hearted hero! . . . Heaven knows what treachery that wolf in sheep's clothing is cooking up for us! . . .

Down to the hold, quick! It may not be too late!

What sitting ducks we'll make if our friend decides to have a little target-practice!

Now, where's he hiding, the gangster!

Thousands of thundering typhoons! There! . . . What did I tell you? . . . Look!

The brute! . . . The cannibal! He's sabotaged the . . . the things . . . er . . . the doings . . . I mean, the whatnots!
Look, a letter.

Great snakes! The poor, poor wretch! . . . This is horrible!
What? What is it? Read it out.

By the time you read this I shall have left the rocket . . .
When I am gone, I hope you will have enough oxygen to reach earth alive.
Perhaps by some miracle I shall escape too.
Forgive me for the harm I have done you —
Wolff

What! It can't be true! If he'd opened the outer door the motor would have stopped.
Wait, there's some more . . .

P.S.
To open the outer door without sounding the alarm and stopping the motors, I had to cut a few wires.
You only need to reconnect them, and everything will work properly again
W.

Ten thousand thundering typhoons! He has gone out into space to save our lives! . . . And I accused him . . .
Yes, Captain. But even so, perhaps his sacrifice will be in vain . . . You go on up. I'll just repair these wires . . .

Ah, there you are. Well, have you caught that thug Wolff?
?

What? What did you say? Wolff a thug?! If ever I hear you say one disrespectful thing about that hero, I'll throw you into space to join him! You understand, you iconoclast, you?!

At that moment . . .
Earth to Moon-Rocket . . . Stand by . . . Ten minutes to go before the turning operation.
Right.

A quarter of an hour later . . .
Earth to Moon-Rocket . . . Turning operation successfully accomplished. Don't give in! In less than two hours you will be back on the Earth.

Yes! . . . And they'll give us an impressive memorial! I can see it from here! To Captain Haddock, a martyr in the cause of Science, etcetera, etcetera!

Well, if I have to die, then at least let it be in the way I choose, blistering barnacles!
Captain! What are you going to do?

What am I going to do? Thundering typhoons, I'm going to empty this bottle of whisky! Alcohol is a poison that kills slowly, they say . . . As slowly as it likes . . .

. . . so as far as I am concerned! It can take its time. I'm in no hurry!

That's enough, Captain! Go and lie down. This is no time to get drunk! . . .

Blistering barnacles, why not? Was I or was I not told that the spirits on board were reserved for an emergency? Well, wasn't I? . . .

It's a thousand to one that we're going to end up as a crate of kippers! Ten thousand thundering typhoons, isn't that an emergency?!

Captain, I would remind you that drunkenness on the public highway is against the law. Go and lie down!

You . . . you two . . . ect-ectoplasms! . . . They needed two P-P-Punch-and-Judy men on the p-p-pier . . . You-you sh-sh-should have stayed there . . .

This time we demand an apology!
Yes, we apologise on demand!

F-f-four to one . . . I . . . I . . . give . . . give up . . .

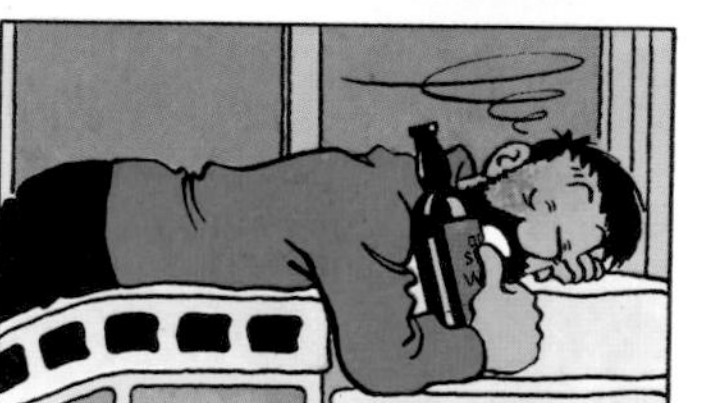

Half-an-hour later . . .
Moon-Rocket to Earth . . . The air's becoming unbreathable . . . The last cylinder from the space-suits has been used up . . . The others are already unconscious . . . I wonder if we can possibly get back alive.

This is Baxter . . . Hang on, Tintin! You have only about fifty thousand miles to go . . . just about another hour. Courage, Tintin! Don't lose heart! . . . All will be well!

Thanks . . . Mr Baxter . . . I'll do my best . . . to hold on till . . . the end . . . but I . . . I . . .

I'm afraid . . . I . . . shan't have . . . the strength . . . Goodbye! . . . Goodbye!

Goodbye! Yes, it's goodbye! May you all perish up there! Jorgen and Wolff bungled their work. We shall not get your accursed rocket . . . Well, may you go to the devil in it! . . .

For nearly an hour the rocket hurtles on towards the Earth.
Earth to Moon-Rocket . . . Stand by . . . You have only about 8,000 miles to go . . . Get ready to set the automatic pilot . . .

Moon-Rocket . . . to Earth . . . Tintin here . . . I understand . . . I . . . I'll try . . . to rouse . . . the . . . Professor.

Professor! Professor! . . . We're nearly home . . . Wake up . . . We've got to . . . set the automatic pilot . . .

Professor! For goodness' sake! . . . Professor please . . . It . . . it's no good . . . I can't rouse him . . . Now what's to be done?

I've . . . I've simply got to . . . try . . . myself . . . There's no one but me . . . Oh, I'm stifling . . .

I must . . . I must get to . . . to the ladder . . .

I've done it . . . But . . . shall I ever have the strength . . .

This . . . awful . . . dizziness!

Earth to Moon-Rocket . . . Are you in the control cabin?
Come on . . . one last effort . . .

Earth calling . . .
I'm nearly . . . there . . .

Earth to Moon-Rocket . . . Earth to Moon-Rocket . . . Hurry up and set the automatic pilot . . . Earth to Moon-Rocket . . . Can you hear me?

Moon-Rocket . . . Can you hear me? . . . Moon-Rocket!

Earth to Moon-Rocket . . . Can you hear me? . . . For heaven's sake answer! . . . There's not a moment to lose! . . . You are plunging to disaster!

Earth to Moon-Rocket! In heaven's name, Tintin, answer!

It's hopeless. He must have passed out. Quick, Walter, make a tuning signal, as piercing as you possibly can . . . It's the only way to bring him back to his senses.
Yes, we can try.

TRIIUUUW

WOOUUIIIIII

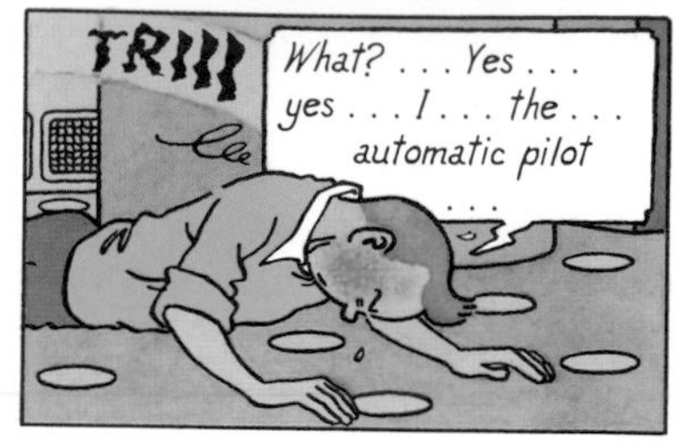
TRIII
What? . . . Yes . . . yes . . . I . . . the . . . automatic pilot . . .

WOOUIIIIIT

I . . . Hello . . . Tintin here . . . Stop . . . the whistling . . . I'm . . . I'm just setting the automatic pilot . . . I . . . I . . . think that's done it . . .
Ah, just in time!

Well done, Tintin . . . Go and lie on your bunk now . . . Have you the strength to do that? . . . Hello Tintin? . . . Hello?

He must have fainted again. Never mind, he's done the essential thing . . . I'll dash over to the landing site now.
Right. We'll keep in touch with you by radio.

Observatory to Control . . . The rocket is only 900 miles from the Earth. In a few moments the auxiliary engine will take over from the nuclear motor.

. . . the rocket is now 550 miles away . . .

That's it . . . The nuclear motor has just cut out. The auxiliary engine will start up in a moment or two . . . But what's happening?

Great Scott! . . . The auxiliary engine hasn't started up . . . The rocket is hurtling towards the ground like a meteor! . . . They're going to be smashed to bits!

Hooray! The auxiliary engine has just started up at last! . . . In twenty minutes the rocket will touch down!
Lets pray they may still be alive!

Meanwhile at the landing site, observers anxiously search the sky for a sight of the rocket.

Look! There she is!

By Jupiter, look! . . . There's a car just setting off across the apron!

By thunder! It's Mr Baxter's car! They obviously can't have seen the rocket coming! They'll risk it falling right on top of them . . . they'll be flattened . . . or roasted!

Hurry up, driver . . . We must be well under cover before the rocket lands!

Help! The rocket! Stop, driver, stop!! . . .

TSIIIII

Fire engines calling . . . The rocket has just landed . . .
Mr Baxter's car is hidden from us by a thick cloud of smoke! . . .

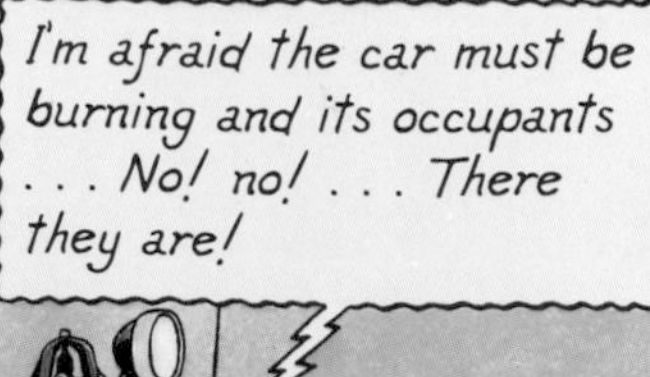
I'm afraid the car must be burning and its occupants . . . No! no! . . . There they are!

Ah, Mr Baxter! What a terrible fright you gave us! . . . Not hurt? . . . No burns . . . ?
No, nothing . . . But the rocket . . . Call the rocket!

Calling Moon-Rocket . . . You have landed! . . . Open the door . . . Moon-Rocket? . . . Moon- Rocket?

Moon-Rocket . . . The gantries are being moved into position . . . Moon-Rocket, I repeat, open the door!

No answer . . . We must cut open the hull . . . Bring the electric saws.

A few minutes later . . .
Hurry! . . . Hurry!

There, that's done it!

Now for the door of the air-lock! This one can be opened from the outside!

There . . . Heavens, not a sound! I feel as if I'm entering a tomb . . .

Professor! . . . Tintin! . . . Captain! . . .

Are we too late? Not a single movement! Hello! HELLO!

Professor! . . . Here, Professor! . . . Professor! . . . It's no good.

Take them into the fresh air at once, and give them oxygen! . . . Hurry! . . . I'll take care of Tintin: he must be up in the control cabin . . .

A few minutes later . . .
Success! He's opening his eyes . . .

I . . . where am I . . . What's happened? . . . The rocket . . .
Don't worry now . . . You're safe and sound . . . back on Earth.
42138

Safe and sound . . . Back on Earth? . . . On Earth? . . . Is it really true? . . . But the others? . . . And Snowy?
The Professor and the detectives are out of danger. So is Snowy . . . But . . .
But? . . .

Your friend the Captain . . . alas, his condition is far more serious . . . and I fear . . .
What are you trying to say? . . . Where is he?

He's over there . . . on that stretcher.
Good heavens!

The Captain! . . . It's not possible! . . . Captain!

Captain! . . . Captain! . . . It's me, Tintin . . . Please, please wake up! . . . We're back home . . . Captain! Captain!

No sign of life . . . Do you really believe that . . .
Alas! His pulse is very irregular, and very weak . . .

But what more can you expect? . . . The man's heart is worn out. But it's not surprising, if what they tell me is true. It seems that he was a great whisky drinker.

What? . . . That wasn't a dream! . . . I distinctly heard it. Someone here just mentioned whisky!!

Captain! My dear Captain! . . . Saved! . . . Heavens, what a fright you gave us!
A fright? You didn't really believe brave old Captain Haddock was going to let himself be snuffed out, did you? Now then, where is that whisky?

Ah, my dear friends! . . . What an adventure! What an adventure!
Here comes the conqueror of the Moon!

Cuthbert! . . . Let me shake your hand, old friend!
Well, Snowy! That's the narrowest escape we've ever had!

Here is the whisky you ordered, sir.
Hooray!

A glass for me too, Captain. I want to drink a toast with you! It's the first time in my life I have tasted this beverage. But this is not the moment to drink camomile tea!
And how!

My friends, we have just lived through the greatest epic of all time: the marks of our feet are inscribed upon the surface of the Moon. And shall we let the dust of centuries hide those glorious marks for ever, gentlemen?

No, that will never be! For I promise you that we shall return there!
!

What? Us go back there? To the Moon? Me go back to the Moon?!

May I be turned into a bollard, blistering barnacles, if I so much as set foot in your flying coffin again! Never, d'you hear? You interplanetary goat, you! Never!!

I tell you, I've learned just one thing from all this: MAN'S PROPER PLACE . . .

?
42138

. . . IS ON DEAR OLD EARTH!

THE END